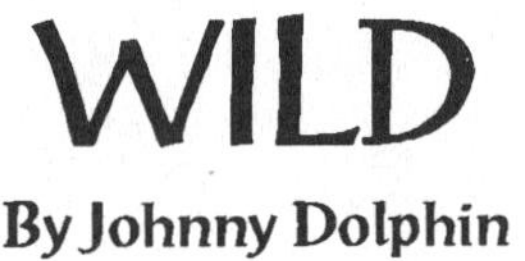

Poems, Aphorisms, and Short Stories

First Edition.
Published by Synergetic Press, Inc.
Post Office Box 650, Oracle, Arizona 85623

Edited by Kathelin Hoffman Gray
Cover illustration by Andy Rush
Book design by K.M. Horton

ISBN 0 907791 26 3

Printed in the United States of America.

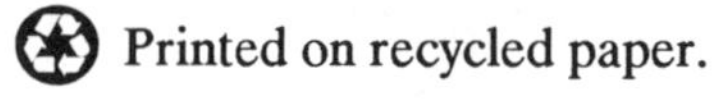

Table of Contents

POEMS

APHORISMS

SHORT STORIES

". . . and on my way rejoicing."

William Burroughs

Poems

Wild

I cheered the skunk
Who challenged Malone
For possession of the porch
Though his death would be decreed
By immutable self-defense;
I watched, crouching in the arroyo,
The deer tearing at the pistachio leaves
While Margret prepared the golden hounds
To drive them onward;
The diamondbacks migrate inward
To pose their menace
By the graveled paths
But all of us refuse
To hunt them down
Beyond the grounds;
The tusked javalina, stalwart, silent,
Looms almost invisible,
Shaded from the moonlight
Beneath the abundant mesquite,
Next to the packrat mansion;
I fall for the girl
Who can't be handled,
The boy who runs away
From being calf-roped and cut into shape,
The woman who glides
Naked without a companion,
Happy in her own skin
Throughout a hidden night,
The man who will quit his power,
Cheerfully walk a lonely path,
Rather than break his contact;
I contemplate the tree root

Overturning the sidewalk,
Breaking-up the pavement,
Eating the jutting rock,
Destroying our kitchen drainage;
I hasten to see the blue crane
Seizing without a thought
My favorite catfish lurking
In our scenic pond,
Then wing away without a glance;
The coyote always on the alert;
The owl ready to swoop;
The artist refusing to produce
Without insight, passion and technique;
The scientist who won't publish
Without something to say
And the necessity to say it;
The manager who can watch
Without getting on people's backs,
Take a break and laugh,
Go broke or make a million
And never lose his touch;
The adventurer who can sit in the shade
And stay out of dusty glory,
Make his moves at the crack of dawn,
And disappear at the right time and place;
The mystic who can strike camp
Like a nomad,
Or by himself, like a troupe of actors,
Strike his set,
Move to new iconographies
And always contemporary performances;
The philosopher who resumes
And presumes, never assumes,
Interrogates himself

More harshly than the Cosmos
And far more harshly than others,
Throws his latest self away
When he's finished with it
As garbage for intellectual compost;
The universe scattered in space,
Lost in time,
Daringly manifest,
Biding eternities behind event horizons,
Point boundaries past envisionable frontiers;
The coruscating spine
That reveals nothing in movement;
The solar plexus sending out
Hormonal signals for ecstasy
To remotest capillarian cell;
Sensation, amplified, intensified, unified,
That apprehends ever new phenomena
Without reaching in any direction
The remotest intimation of a limit;
The material brain in electronic symbiosis
With energetic mind to refine
Ever-more refined transforms,
Soul upon soul,
Some, so informally ethereal as to be
Perhaps capable of cosmic immortality,
But nonetheless, also abandoned
After being experienced,
Because I'm mad with the love
Of unknowable perfume,
The ever creating, ever destroying, ever living
Wild.

The Wildcat

My lean Sioux buddy, Eddie,
Said to me one evening
While we sat around an ironwood fire
Wedged into a small stand of honey mesquite,
Searing steaks wrapped with bacon,
Savoring the cold desert on our backs,
"I came back to my cabin,
Opened the door,
And saw this wildcat staring at me.
I shot him between the eyes,
He went rigid
But he didn't fall for a long time.
He glared at me,
His four legs, stiff, holding him up
Although he couldn't move.
He tried to kill me with his eyes.
Suddenly he fell like a log, completely.
That's what I call wild."

The Survival of Thought

The biggest silent camouflaged,
Ruthlessly cunning most charming predators
Hang out in the library
Ready to pounce on unwary
And delicious flesh
To re-incarnate their motionless attention.
Beyond Good and Evil
I zoom down the Open Road
Past the Possessed and their snakelike claws,
Feast at the Symposium's banquet;
Later, in Cities of the Red Night
I hear Naked Lunches slurped.
The Process creates a magic Tempest;
The Origin of Species
Throws sinister light on War and Peace
And Men Without Women's White Fang
Illuminates Life on the Mississippi.
I slowly somersault backwards
Over the Book of the Dead
Into Metamorphoses of You Can't Go Home Again
Until the Escaped Cock
Heats up the Tropic of Cancer
Into fugues of Four Quartets.
Revelations of Genesis
Burn the Tree of the Kabbalah
And the Journey to the North
Ends in a Hundred Years of Solitude
Making Love in the Time of Cholera
While Capital transforms the Wealth of Nations
Into Patterns of Culture and Grapes of Wrath;
Spaceship Earth orbits the Empire of the Sun;
Up from the Ape

Confronts Information Theory;
The Genetic Code
Engages in Research on Lost Times;
Flowers of Evil
Float away Traces of Bygone Biospheres,
And the Search for Extraterrestrial Intelligence
Runs on a reef in the Heart of Darkness
Where She contemplates Alchemy and
The Periodic Table.
The Inspector General searches the Cherry Orchard
For the time When We Dead Awaken;
Man and Superman in Armies of the Night
Alternate between Vanity Fair
And Secrets of the Great Pyramid.
Dizzy under the blows of the Critique of Pure Reason,
The World as Will and Idea.
Fuses to the Plumed Serpent,
Until All and Everything,
The Jewel of Ahbor Valley,
Becomes real from Meetings With Remarkable Men
And the Search for the Miraculous
Hears and obeys the Call of the Wild.

Storm Along the Gila

In the blackest night
Thunder
Lightning
Mountains.
Quickly into the bosque of mesquite.
Though only shrub on windy slopes,
Mesquite rivals oak
Rooted in wide arroyos' watery sands.
Safe in that oasis forest
I watch the lightning
Reveal the Sonora
The original sound and light show.
The barbed cholla
Iconic opuntia
Ever-ready catsclaw;
Ears open
For flash flood
Hanging loose close to the
Escape path up the arroyo's bank.
The air turns sweet
From ions reversing charge
Wind gusts over the cooling sand,
Sharp rain arrives
A lover's fingernails.
I chew a strip of jerky
Stick my tongue out
Catch a drink
From the twig's drip
A crystal
Storing up inner lightning.

The Trap

It's through our weak
and short attention
That we're ridiculed and ice-creamed
To domesticate ourselves
To where the house cat seems free.
The last thing even
Those who strengthen attention
Care to study
Are the details
Of the cycles of our behavior;
The recurrence of these cycles
Without observation/investigation
Of the details of our complicity
Convince us of their objective reality
Although actually we learned them
Step by arduous step
Till the trap sprung.

The Tiger of Biosphere 2

In a hundred and eighty tons of air
Its carbon dioxide prowls;
Lashing a tail on a stormy night
It picks up one hundred and fifty kilograms;
During the lazy hot day following the front
It exhales the same back into the green surround,
King of the three acre domain,
Striped with daily ups and downs.

In the Rainforest

Life lives so abundantly on top
Bathing in sunshine
Gulping rain in bromeliad containers
That it darkens the ground
Where living columns
Supporting buttressed architecture
Co-evolve gliding gargoyle sculptures.
The Rainforest transpires daily moisture
Straight up on the rising air
Until meeting the roof of its roof,
cold stratosphere,
Rain forms again, falls straight down
Bringing nitrogen with its lightning,
Culling out old trees with surgical strikes;
The Rainforest learned to live rich off poverty,
Off red leached soil empty of fertile mineral,
Iron and aluminum heavy clays all that's left,
By making tough large leaves,
Dropping them in dainty heaps on the barren clay,
Gossamer roots cycling them back up the trunks,
Managing two million square miles of climate;
Branches of the great boles
Work vast sciences of chemical invention
To support this autarchic economy,
Foods, dyes, poisons, cures,
Mind-cosmoses, taste-delights, eye-wonders;
The Rainforest defends itself with fevers, nightmares,
Assassinations, and disorienting highs
From invaders carrying madness, greed and war,
But most of all, by a beauty that makes us stop,
Take oath to protect her.

The Ocean in Biosphere 2 Goes Wild

The anemone slowly shifts location
Until it catches the most, most easily
Of what it needs.
Day after day I watch it in the back reef,
Sometimes tentacles resting within itself,
Sometimes stretched out in full extension, oscillating.
The parrot fish grows noticeably bigger by the week,
The ones weighing more than a pound eat too much,
They'll have to be hunted out.
The thin orange sponges on the fore reef
Expand their area.
The conches determinedly mow through the algae
Headed toward the thickest growths.
The water becomes clearer
As the nitrate fluctuates to around 10 ppb,
The nitrite to about 5 ppb.
The sea grass waves in bottom reaches of the tide
The way prairie grass does in wind
But with slower periods.
The pH begins to hover at 8.0, buffered by carbonate.
Powerful sunlight drives through the water
Forming swaying columns, translucent portals of energy
Disappearing into green increase.
The brain coral hefts its slow sure growth.
Sea urchins gleam by the purple fan corals.
Angel fish dive down a small oxygen rich cell
To hang out for their tooth cleaner's arrival.
Microbiota and snails increase by scads.
The crab hunts decisively that
Which it was bred and selected to find.
The ocean remains invisible;
Its visible glories live and die;

Its physico-chemical functions register
Repeatable numbers;
After a year's observations, I begin to swim
With its shadow.

Sound Bites from A Presidential Campaign

The farmers may be blown away
But our flag factories make more money than ever
Our girls may be raped
But they must bear the children for
The sterile rich to select
To stick their name on
So they can will their money
To their fake immortality
And the unselected ones
Can swell the struggling population
To keep the wages down.
Our cities may have exploded
Into a zoning catatonia
But we'll drop the speculation tax
To fifteen percent
To increase the incentive
To sell America out at a 100% profit.
Everybody on drugs
Will be kicked out of athletics,
The army, the navy, the schools,
Unless, of course,
They are members of the CIA
Experimenting with a friendly dictator,
And you must pledge allegiance
To fakery and boredom

And never question me in public
And why should you ever ask a question
You've never had it so good
You've never had it better,
Nobody ever had it better,
This is all you can expect
And besides, if you want anything else
Anything else at all
You must be a
LIBERAL LIBERAL LIBERAL LIBERAL.

"Erase the Shame!"

Voltaire

The hate filled faces
Of fundamentalist grunts
Mobbing and jeering
In their fanatic hunts.
The young brave girls
With pregnant deserted flanks
Have to run the gauntlet
To fight for their chance.

My Enemy

A thousand acres of wattle to chop;
I counted a million down the first year
And ninety acres looked clear;
Three others had helped me,
Two months, eight hours a day
Till hand toughened and loose shoulders loosened;
Next year half of those wattle surged again;
I stopped counting, elaborately visualized;
Ten years after I chopped
Around that field in two hours
But altogether only six hundred acres had been won,
In four hundred the wattle battled on.
Seeds in Savannah
Fight a long term strategic war
Against drought, flood, fire, termite and man;
They keep a ten year supply
Dispersed in soil, throw only a fraction
Into each year's chances;
The next year of the ones triggered to thrust,
If even a relative few escape their foes,
They fully stock the paddock again.
Plants arrived long before us,
They survived and flourished
Through disasters no man could live through;
Our neighbors stopped their trucks
To laugh at my chopping,
Back raising and lowering like a machine,
But the wattle, that invader,
That moved into this area
With the sheep's overgrazing
Native grasses for fifty years,
That wattle aroused precise ferocity;

I had found a life or death position;
My friends, of course, brought in tractors,
Brought in chain plows,
But wattle grew better than ever
In that disturbed, thin, sandy soil,
Remnant of a Permian desert, epochs ago,
What with the annual monsoon
Drenching lusty roots
Followed by long fervent sunshine.
Finally, my friends joined the campaigns
with the same precise ferocity;
We chopped up, down, around the paddocks,
Became connoisseurs of termite mounds,
Branches on which cockatoos would congregate,
Of how the Birdwood and Buffel clumped,
The differing shade of Ghost Gum, Baobab
Or Bloodwood
Among the heat-drenched miles
Where no quarter was given.
Some roots thrust back
Three times, three years running, to make new wattle;
Each time the root hardened, lengthened, stiffened;
Sometimes, exhausted, my adze bounced strengthlessly
Off three inch thick ironlike roots,
Aimed back at my leg by those hostile veterans.
I laughed at last with a loping stride
And dazzling swing with complete follow through
Because I grew wilder than wattle;
Wattle was going to retreat;
I found a place inside equal to wattle's power.
The roll call of the Nine Paddocks
That divided the thousand acres
Had in ten years of struggle
Become mantrams containing aboriginal power;

I call them off:
Boab
Pioneer
New Trail
Disaster
Polo
Pump
Twin Gums
Paradise and
Victory.
I gaze across the boundary at tens of thousands
Of wattle looming for the few miles that I can see
Of the ten thousand square miles I know they rule,
And salute a most splendid enemy
Ever ready to take all my winnings back;
My immanent-transcendent enemy
Has been my most faithful ally
My most extraordinary teacher.
Galaxy begins to fill the sky.
Small field hawks sweep by my head.
Blood runs sweet as immortality.

Love Your Enemies

Love your enemies because
They not only remorselessly attack
Or expose to attack
Any of your weak points
So that you not only can but
Must change them,
But they lie and make up
New faults that do not yet even
Exist,
But could,
Without vigilance;
And so, allow you to
Change your future for the better.
All of the above, of course,
Assumes that you can survive their
calculated onslaughts.

April 1991

When attacked and wounded
The coyote slinks back to his hole
Using the principle of least action
To lick the spots where he bleeds.
Poetry is my hole;
I bound out when healed,
I recuperate within it when scarred,
I disappear in it when the baying hounds sniff near,
Alone then, anonymous, too invisible to bother,
In that vaster-than-we-can-ever-dream formless
From which forms emerge in pulses, dazzling,
To direct astonishing existential displays,
Concatenating objects, practical and symbolic,
Then leave the stage
To rest in the magic green room of potentiality.
Already, tonguing word spittle into essence cuts,
My mind-blood's flow's clotted and staunched,
My lips curl in loose coyote grin,
Once more I prowl zig-zag the scudding moon,
Effortlessly missing prickly pear and jumping cholla,
Invisible to the hunters looking for my head.

The Hunt

The coyotes
Bounced their subtle a cappella jazz
Off the cactus strewn cliff;
In the moon-filled night,
Laser and I bounded after them
Down the steep slope
Through the stickly thorned clawed
Without getting a scratch
Silently gliding in on their voice trail
Leading us to the white sanded arroyo
And the blue gramma grassed bank
Under the heat and drought curved mesquite
Where they had howled in combo moments before.
We occupied their ancient space, cross-legged,
Waving our oncoming companions to sit in a circle
Eyes reflecting the reflected fires in the sky
Wolfing it all in,
A small pack on the loose
Who had found a spot
Where action flickered and flared.

Who Am I?

I am the youthful loose-limbed blue dancing Krishna seducing country girls to far-out dreams;

I am the westerner strolling towards the sunset ready to touch off the experimental biosphere on the Mars-facing launching pad;

I am the gambling Tibetan quaffing barley fermented chang, innerly repeating mantrams until the yantra of archons operate my one-pointed mind through a corpse-filled phenomenology;

I am the romantic girl who refuses to compromise on her desire for total satisfaction on every level, gazing, wide-green-eyed, toward paintings never painted, novels never written, ideas never whispered, men never born;

I am the engineer calculating the tolerances and safety factors on intricate interlocks of dynamic systems of differing scales, life spans, stabilities, materials, energies, costs, and logistical problems surrounded by books of standards, computers networked to genius, and problems galore;

I am the manager watching illusions, neuroses, ambitions, cultural patterns shifting by, waiting for the intersections with reality, when decision can intervene against disaster or victoriously seize opportunity unseen in the general melee for scarce resources, or retreat to fight again;

I am the mystic who has talked with the dead, heard dazzling commands and inexorable truths, my body pushed again and again to explosion's brink by invisibly powerful breaths, prolonged sweats, rigid strengths, and can never speak without lying and am a master of camouflage;

I am the guy who forgets everything and always wonders what it's all about and always has to start again from the bottom, believes anything and everything, the perpetual sucker, who only saves his ass by always moving on;

I am the old son-of-a-bitch who's seen it all, done it all, been there, come back, and insouciantly thinks all is one dangerous delight hiding behind scarecrow masks of terror, despair, and pleasure;

I am the coach choleric at any and all forms of stupidity and incompetence on the part of the players and unfairness on the part of the referees and sometimes I rage at the top of my voice but I never forget the game plan or to improve the material on my team, though sometimes I get thrown off the field or fired out of town or there's a hot new job offer;

I am the actor fascinated by the astonishing world, who has to initiate action in all its disguises and make the inner motive and the historic pressure clear to the puzzled audience leaning hopefully forward, and there is no role too small to reveal the play, its transcendental stakes;

I am the ship of fools, bare-masted, swept toward green-blue cliffs of ice across the savage sixties, or in full sail blown by trade wind twenties toward stick-boomed dances in great thatched huts in dark green coolness far up the river as large as a sea, or careening across the Roaring Forties forever toward the unknowable, short of people, short of skills, and only miracles of synchronicity save the adventure.

No One Escapes But Some Do It Better

An adventurer without expeditions,
An artist without performances,
A scientist without experiments,
A philosopher without a critique,
A manager without a project,
A mystic wanders a road without a road.

At night the gravel path serves for sleeping,
Dry bread for steak, its crust for chocolate,
Solitude becomes intenser than high politics,
Starlight more penetrating than poetry,
Death, it's clear, is the only game in town,
But timing calls all the shots.

Off, Off and Away

Try to push back a flood—
Sloshes right through your fingers,
Rises to rumble you away;
Try to push back a storm,
Howls right through your wool,
Sleets, hails to blow you away;
Lurid lightning stalks
The Santa Catalina Mountains,
Shattering the giant old willow,
Splitting the guardian granite rock.
Fire, water, wild,
I, too, scud canyons, ranches and mines,
Surf solar winds,
Sail the backside of time
In translunar expeditions.

Litany to the Names of Allah

The eagles of subtlety
Soar cliffs of the sublime
In which we read libraries of the learned
And discern our way past palaces of the able
Past temples of beauty
To encampments of truth
Which hunt the wilderness of the subsistent
At whose center sits the one
Upon his throne of mercy
Who can gallop to the frontiers of compassion
Where with hope of the most high
He will welcome arrival of the friend
With music of the all-hearing
Dances of the all-seeing
And act together in dramas of the guide
Burned by the always new of the greater
In red heartbeats of the ever-living
Toward seven worlds of the creative
Where who-can-say grapples with what-might-be
In Nowheresville, the deeply hidden.
Occasionally, a feather from one of those eagles
Flutters to the well-plowed and many peopled
Plains of China,
Arousing a heedless one to remember to
Remove his ignorance.

How 1

To reconstitute the worlds
From nothing
Again, again, again,
Each time freshly new
Ah, that's the secret
To escape the darkest prison
The dreariest chore
The dullest job
The boringest thought
The dumbest emotion
The most wearied sensation
The most authoritarian tradition
The most unfeeling logic
The most tyrannical state
The most witchhunting media
The most repetitious argument
The most dangerous confrontation
The most destructive symbol
The most hypocritical gesture
The most blah language
The most folly-filled ecstasy
The most profitless activity
The most insolent socialite,
The most resentful mob
The most pompous professional
The grimmest street scene
The one can do that secret —
Wild, man.

How 2

Nobody gonna attain wild
Who didn't make it free,
Nobody gonna get free
Without a fight,
Nobody gonna win a fight
Who don't reach no street smart.
Nobody gonna zing street smart
Who don't get hip
Nobody gonna get hip
Till they stop feeling for themselves
And start lookin' around themselves
Nobody gonna look around because of death
As long as they scared to death,
Nobody gonna get brave enough to start
Thinking they get killed if they start
They gotta never say die
Nobody gonna ever say never say die
Till they dance with wild
And make out with wild.

How 3

I was happy I made free
Till I asked what do I be?
Just escaped dog skulking
Just old ruin hulking.
How to find wolf once more
How to renew with it lore,
How to find others to see stars
How to turn my spine from bars
And lope through cactus nights
Not depending on city lights?
How to go past poems and muses,
Without regret blow the fuses
Power myself from sex to god,
Eliminate cringe from rod?
There's in quick what's very quick
You gotta finesse to get in your lick,
To make your trail in night
Out of mind and out of sight.

Expedition

Reality
Charges ahead
Playing Go games
Speaking, Painting
Landscaping, Breeding
Establishing
Designing, Calculating
Constructing, Demolishing
Killing, Healing
Teaching Acting Classes
Studying, Publishing
Montaging Multi-Media Hypertexts
Contemplating its switching tail
With tawny eyes
Keen not to miss any gest
Of its own self-astonishing moves.

Tell Me All the Places You Been

I been to so many places.
Tell me.
So many places I haven't been.
Ulan Bator and grave of Genghiz Khan.
Angkor Wat and stage of the school of dance.
Moulay Idries and cliff of the secret singers.
Alamout and soma of transmutation
Mount Kailas and spot that is center.
Chang-An and elucidation of ineluctables.
The Himalayan hut and shamans' spirit trail.
The Street called Straight and way called crooked.
The Palace of Knossos and bull-guarded labyrinth.
Mahabalipuram and origin of I.
Shanghai and jade statue that overturned the
Mandate of Heaven.
The caves of Amu Darya and reed of ecstasy.
Samothrace and tantra of the Goddess.
The Samoyeds and architectures of schizophrenia.
Chivor and clairvoyance of its green fires.
You seen everyplace else?
Some places I don't even know about.
Does anybody know about them?
Perhaps no one knows these places.
Where humanity began and how it survived.
Where life began and how it arrived.
Where worlds intersect and disappearances succeed.
Where wisdom first danced and how she strips off.
Where language began and chanted the first poem.
Where death, sex, and power
First stirred their alchemical vat.
Where understanding will commence
And intelligence navigate with time space and life.

Vertebrate 'X'

We will move again through the air-water ocean like
The great whales, but this time in co-regulated
Air-water oceans that will meiosis time and again,
Populating space and time, building up improbable
Concentrations of energy until the secrets of
'Big banging' and 'black Holes' are fully revealed.
What a multi-level dyad!
From Cosmology to Freud
Physics to Metaphysics.
Between the Big Bang
And the Black Holes
Arise a hundred billion galaxies
Each with a hundred billion stars
Each with a hundred billion biospheres
Each with a hundred billion dreams
Each with a hundred billion bits
All facing death
All facing the one-in-a-million
Long shot for transcendence
The long roam throughout
    The Unknowable
    The Unbeable
    The Understandable
    But not Uncontactable
Until Impossibility itself
    Becomes a local option
And biospheres co-regulate
    The Multiverse,
    The Cosmos,
    The Wild,
And we stream in and out
    Of sunlit local gases
    On our sensors of delight

At the same time collecting and recollecting Memory
For that Shipwreck moment
When we need it all and then some
To keep the voyage going going
And never gone.

The Artist

Gold, silver and space,
Yoshida's face before his face;
Down those golden curves we run
In silver orbits of the sun;
His two-dimensional glow
Create a multi-vectored flow;

As we gaze into the chemistry,
We are pulled into a mystery;
Old Yoshida somehow did it
But how? How well he hid it!

Effect and Cause

We made merry before champagne came;
We howled before the moon arose;
We fell in love before the veil of beauty dropped;
We spent millions before the cash flow started;
We danced before the fiesta arrived;
We made poems before the curtain rose.

Late September 1988

Elevation 3900 feet

32 degrees N

110 degrees W

Harvest moon shone on haystack after haystack of sensations; sowed, ripened and mown in each eighteenth of a second perceptual frame. The cicadas micro-increased frequency and pitch, exulting in their species' discovery: a million-yeared econiche amongst those energy transformations that upgrade a micro-fraction of inputted electromagnetic radiation to passionate intelligent dreams that can allow millions of manifestations.

The ingeniously recycled waterfall held algae population to reasonable mass equilibrium in the gleaming pond created by a dam calculated to change the flash flood to reflective mood;

Then, I took you, sweeter than the sweetness of the ripened plum sugar, each caress petalling a tantric rose, forever fragrant in a mantric pose;

And I hurled, and I hurl that moment throughout the endless and numberless undifferentiated eternities of my enemy and his armies without, accidents and diseases, and traitors within, feckless and reckless;

And my enemy's attack turns into green cosmic mirrors, backstage and carnival mirrors, microscopic and telescopic mirrors, cracked mirrors and bartender's mirrors, and the mirror that Orpheus and Brion Gysin walked through, revealing in bizarre, sudden, surprising, opulent, infinite glimpses the midnight secret that will live as long as this;

And do not regret that you will forget, I will forget, she will forget, poetry disappear, our species give way, even our genus subside beneath a host of superior forms brought forth by cosmic struggle with billion-yeared time, because contemplation will receive yet more magnificent munificence;

But that late September night was a necessary step upon the way.

In the Caravan of Dreams

In the Caravan of Dreams
Mystery haunts the House.
The trumpet player behind the bar
Riffs into the blonde eyes of the waitress
Fifteen minutes early to work
Prowling the setting for the night's sets.
On the great mural
Blue and red lights flow and flop
Visions of Yoruban drums torn from
Trancemaker's hands,
Battered horns handed out, slave owners derision,
For slaves to celebrate their dead
But, deprived of the talking drums,
The mourners no longer bring down Shango;
Then, from death's after-taste in brothels
Whose waves outrolled the Mother of Waters
Keened out slop and slide and wail,
Gaunt half tones trembling even upper vertebrae
While the bass beat marks
Action's quanta
From which hip delight,
Rare, far-out emotions,
Smoke, burn, then incandesce
Down chaotic bifurcating time,
Resonant, insistent, penetrating sub-octaves.
Sound distilled the audience
To screams and breathlessness.
We switch our tails,
Lions surrounding the waterhole
Where thirst drives
All we need to devour.

Cool

Rage
Is not wild
But a predictably deadly hand grenade of emotion;
Screaming
Is not wild
But a predictably regressing physiological release;
Wild
Is the blue haze
Of the Rainforest emanating its isoprenes
To
Precipate the rains,
The thunderous lightning that restores its nitrogen;
Wild
Is the bleaching coral
Cutting down its colorful algae
To
Survive the increased heat
Gaining the best chance to live till temperature changes;
Wild
Is the cosmic ray
Hitting the exact point of genetic mutation
To
Put out another candidate
Who could be elected to a million year term of office;
Wild
Is the Unpredictable
Elegantly integrating
Yet another guise into the matrix of danger.

Adventure

Beneath the jutting cliff of Aphrodite,
Waiting, alert, the mysterious cave open
For those whose ships sail craftily in
And drop their anchors
To rise and fall with the tides
Taking time to search out treasures
Both buried and not yet mined,
Waiting especially for daring Odysseus's ship.
That cave built hygiene and panacea
Full of charms, music, and divine dance
For one witty enough to leave it timely
But turning into pigs all those who overstay.
Ah, Odysseus, precisely patient,
Ruthlessly charming, artistically sly, sweetly reasonable,
Could survive war, disgrace, love, ocean, and exile
And depart victor from his public appearance.
Silent himself, his stories resonate from Homer's lips;
He was never caught in any web
That either he or other wove.

Outback

Cruel wind blew out our tracks
Where we laughed upon our backs;
White cockatoos creak by
With wise and happy cry;
They feel group immortal,
I feel brief individual;
I wish what each poet desires:
Unending fragrant fires,
Unending your two kisses,
Unending tumultuous blisses,
Unending roaring touch,
Your gifts never too much;
It's you I wish to love
Not astral up above.
Oh, how I'd punch Time out,
If I could find that lout.

Zing

Stars in the sky
Glints in your eye
Never will I
Know more than this
Not in a kiss
Nor bursting bliss.

Zingles

Each kiss and stroke a snowflake
A slow storm each different and each perfect
Life's water stored in equations of crystalline gravity
Benign chaos drifting upon heavily seeded earth.

La Rose de Provins

Rosa Gallica
"Rosa de Charlemagne"
Cosmetique, alimentaire,
  horticoles, pharmaceutiques.
Petales: Infusions, lotions, gargarisms ¤
  l'eau de rose carmine collyre

Vinca Minor — La Petite Peovenche
Infusions tonique, carmine astringent
  in the camp of philtres d'amour

Acanthus Mollis
  "Architectural motifs"

La Rose de Damas
La Rose de Damas
  trés odorante
Copper and rope handrail

Power of Memory

Thick grape bursting
 sweetly between lip and teeth,
Full moon lit up my
 summer's meander
 through the apricots, peaches, and pears,
My feet cooled in
 damp wiry blue gramma grass,
Slow wind slid
 beneath my unbuttoned shirt,
But remembering you,
 I sunk to my knees
And my eyes
 closed to the beautiful world.

Dialogue

You taught me about love's honor
I taught you about power's truth
You brought me in to life
I took you out to death
You gave me happiness
I showed you nothingness
You made the fire
I turned out the lights.

Recognition

Like the sun
Your head arrived
Above eyes
Full of smoke of seas
Far above your mouth
Where kisses carefully kindling
From the intelligence of love
Warmed the dawn-cool
Priestess of delight
Overlooking the long wheatfields,
The cliff abruptly plunging
To the foam drummed oceanic cave
From which the dancer bounded
On long haunting legs
To become the wave-born
Destruction of the proudest walled city.

Gifts

Your dense green glance
Showers platinum credit cards
On the big-eyed hungry street boy
No wonder
I gave up hustling my ass.

Story

In the beginning was the Flesh,
And the Flesh performed the Deed
That resounded with the Word
And ever since then
Man has had to work his way
Up through the Word and
Then the Deed
To become Flesh and Blood again.
Master of the six Breaths
And the seven-fold Structure
Aligned with the Macrocosmic Flow
Engaged in the supreme Adventure
Where All is forever being decided.
And re-decided
In Stupendous
Mysterious
Dramatic
Danger.

The Trackless

Where Am I?

I am here, there and everywhere
I am outside the universe
I am inside the inside
I am in places yet to be
I am in placed gone from memory
I am in the mutating gene
I am in the frog's splash
I am in the eagle's eyrie
I am in the pack rat's hole
I am in the tiled meditation chamber
I am on the homeless man's cardboard.
I am in front of your nose.

What Am I?

I am nothing
I am no one
I am no man
I am no thought
I am no emotion
I am no sensation
I am no movement
I am no form
I am no end point
I am no beginning
I am no word
I am no symbol

Why Am I?

I am contemplating
I am acting
I am evolving

I am understanding
I am noticing
I am fascinated
I am directed
I am divided
I am remembering
I am choosing
I am deciding
I am committing.

How Am I?

I am mirror
I am light of light of light
I am subtle
I am beautiful
I am powerful
I am able
I am learned
I am hidden
I am friend
I am subsistent
I am alive
I am real

Who Am I?

I am truth
I am eros
I am creativity - destruction
I am destiny
I am Man
I am animal
I am plant
I am soil
I am protein and emerald

I am gold and oxygen
I am electron and photon
I am heat and information

When Am I?

I am before time
I am after time
I am in the whick-whacks of time
I am at time's intersections with decision
I am at the right time
I am at the wrong time
I am in dreamtime
I am in clocktime
I am in scheduled time
I am in deadline time
I am in time out.

Fort Worth Caravan of Dreams

Haunting, Taunting beauty
Stretches, fetches duty.
It strolls, tolls the way
Through facts, acts of day
Past bounds, sounds of sense;
It never, ever relents
But cries, pries me
With hook, crook of be
Past waves, graves of light
To a wrack, black sight
Where lost, tossed, I thrill,
One, won, will.

Libretto for Ornette Coleman

Around a glorious star
Ten planets
Thousands of asteroids
Millions of species
And all human history
Revolve,
Spiralling
That star's cosmic path,
Attracting reinforcements,
Light particles, gravitons,
Carbonaceous solids
Who knows what unknowns,
Those humans
Already sending
Off their first probe
Beyond that star.
The prime creative energy
That awakened a receptive planet,
Stashed with water, carbon, and nitrogen,
Orgasmic with its own volcanoes
And uranic heat
To build prolifering bodies of life
That developed and fed a cosmic mind
Nibbling terabytes of information.
How many worlds
Dance on the tip of that computer?

Johnny and Ornette
reared on opposite sides
Of the Red River,
European, African, and both American,
Ate the same biscuits, gravy,

Fried chicken, blackeyed peas, and sweet potatoes.
The one heard melodies,
The other saw metaphors,
They walked grabbing eyeballs
Down long straight
New York distances.
A new curveball
Thrown at every corner.
Ecstatic after *Naked Lunch*.
Japanese singer
Clicked in.

"That's no accident".
"No, man, at this place
There're no accidents."

In that synchronic attractor
The chaos of their lives made sense,
They dropped defense,
Ate a Korean plate,
Drank Puerto Rican coffee,
Traded glints with an Iroquois,
Fell into eyes,
And laughed at perfumed costumes
Swaying ten degrees past foreplay,
"We gotta do something together"
"We gonna do it"
"Should a done it before."
"What did you really look for
In all your travels — truth?
A woman? Power?"
"I looked for Man."
"You couldn't see no man.
All you coulda seen was men."

"I looked for men who
Manifested Man."
"Talk about it, and I'll
Make the music."

First man I ever met,
Grandad, big, strong, smart,
Everybody else put their head down at prayer,
He held knife upright in left hand,
Fork straight up in right hand,
Ready,
Lookin' straight ahead.
I raised my eyes
Saw what he saw
All the other heads bowed,
My father repeating his prayer
As if thoughtful
But same old words;
Women's heads silent. The moment ended,
Grandad plunged, lightning reach,
Fork into bread and took
Straight to his mouth to bite,
Then piled up his plate.
At the farm I threw the cat
Into the pond,
It howled, furious,
"You throw that cat in?"
"Yessir."
"Look at that pond!"
His boot lifted my seven year behind
Gently as possible delivered the kick,
Splash, face first, angry—
"That's what the cat felt like."
The anger disappeared.

He had two books in simple bedroom,
Bible and complete Shakespeare,
Painting of favorite horse,
Cartoon of pipe-smoking bulldog,
Lots of lightning rods
On the white two-story,
Stop-green shingled house,
Out on the prairie.
He connected the toilet
To the gardens,
Built a smokehouse for potatoes,
Onions, and hams,
Dug a cellar for the canning
And cyclones,
And squirted the cat's mouth
Standing on hind legs ten feet away
The first stream of milk
From his teat of his Jersey Cow
And let me shower
Under the streaming wheat grains
Golden, cool, and hard,
Standing in the combine bin
As he drove the thresher down the bumpy fields
In dazzling hot-blue summer.
He had eight children,
All turned out interesting to a boy,
Uncle Gus and Uncle Polk even heroes,
And Uncle Frank a face
That drew a map of masculine emotion.
Granmaw stood six feet tall
And his sister, Greataunt Jennie,
Weighed three hundred pounds,
The subtlest cook I ever knew,
And that in face

Of heavy competition.
From her brother's wife
And my aunts and mother.
He ran his farms,
Ran his garage,
Ran the New Deal
In his part of the country,
And stayed completely off your back.
He ruled by reinforced respect
Because he could do it
But you could see he
Never believed a word of its reports
And so he never overdid it.
He had survived
The shooting of his last two brothers
At his side
In one of Texas's great feuds.
Tired of killing,
He lit out with Kate
And Jenny north
On the Chisholm Trail
And homestead the Indian Territory,
A Jeffersonian
Who believed in educated people
Controlling their own land
And livelihood.
He never preached,
He let you see him doing.
He drove to the exact speed
Formulas of car and road allowed,
But he walked on foot
The mile to the bank
For the annual loan negotiation
For seed and fertilizer,

And that set the local rate
He died when I turned eight.
He showed me what a man should be,
But I didn't know how he did it;
So I searched the world to
Meet other men to learn that secret.
It's hard to find,
And harder to do.

Potatoes

Root-eyed
Tined from the raked-up mound
Around which limp green
Yellowed to mulch,
I picked you up,
Distinct underworld beings
On my knees following grandmother
The hot sun browning my back,
Fingers and toes slushing
Fresh sticky dirt drying frazzly grey
All I wore blue jeans and moment
We placed the potatoes one-deep
Each sturdy solid potato
On the racks underneath
Bunched onions in the smokeshed—
My grandfather died that summer.

Nineteen

My life's still mostly hope,
Nothing's resolved, I tell myself;
A few images burned on my vision,
A few sentences embedded in my brain.
Beadlike stars adorn the black,
But still half-boy, unbelieving,
Occasionally I leave my desk
To tramp brown winter-hardened hills,
There in pungent pasture grass,
Fief of provincial earth,
To trace through twig-curved sky
And sun-curled verge
The refracted pause of light
That pours remembrance
Through a cloudy heart.
Abandoned the warm hearth
Though hunger came, and drabness,
Dumb violence and weary struggle,
The unromantic sacraments of adventure.
Endless studies . . .
Tired and skeptical eyes,
Confusion, flickering dreams,
Rainbow promises of knowledge.
And unwitting, lying loves,
All love can tell a partner,
Knowing not itself.
I laugh it off, listening
To the lonesome humor of a hound.

Oklahoma May

Sun tousles
Nuzzling air,
I tousle
Your nuzzling hair,
Days work greenly,
Nights stroll fair.

Teasing your breasts,
Teasing your eyes —
The sexual month
Trails dragonflies,
Meadowlarks,
And cloud-white skies.

Your touch trembles,
Swells bold,
Grain heavying,
Heading to gold;
You smile, I laugh,
Joy is foaled.
Love, when wheat
Tinders the plain,
Harvest will fire,
It surges claim;
Fall to, reap,
And seed again!

Bear in the Buckwheat, Turkey in the Beach

Little boy big heart
Lightning thunder
Pounding rain
Hot summer chilling
Flower buttered mud
Water rolling gleaming dark
I don't belong here
I need there
I need a map
I take a long nap;
Five years later
Swaying swinging bridge
Pecan trees tall
Red flood below
Straight cut banks
Nature power
Everybody else inside
I in my hide
I don't belong here
I need there
I need a map
I take another nap;
Tiptoe my feet
Twenty feed above thud
Topping apple trees
My buddy, lean idiot,
"I like your singing".
School teacher said "No Good",
"Hey, come on!"
"Yeah, I do".
I sung some more

My heart wasn't sore
I belong here
I go there
I make a map
Now it's a snap.

Country Afternoon, Yakima

Light, clearer than water,
Splashed on Mount Adam's snow,
Fell on ridging tamarack,
Slid from my neighbor's apples,
Down on drunken bees,
Drowsy and yellow-laden,
Lurching like galleons
From Mexicos of clover;
This light washed out the lines
With which I fenced the world.

Oklahoma

Born under forever frontier sky,
Why stick to dwindling squares
Whose grandfathers scorned horizons,
Why corral ourselves with tired-out words?

When despair settled damp,
Like rust on wheat, discoloring, obscene,
When no good way to save harvest showed,
And a good burning seemed in order,
When even the roots seemed rotting,
I strode alone by swinging river curves
Till I reached the country of the Cheyanne;
Thunder brawled below the moon,
Echoed drunkenly down streaming canyons,
Fell to sleep and dreamed a dream
Like a lariat to lasso white mares.

An old farmer twanging milk in a pail,
Somehow he'd landed from Holland in 1910.
Asked me if I was bound nowhere,
And had me to breakfast on peaches and ham.
But men dream sunsets to match each dawn;
Quick profits plowed the bluestem;
From frame alleys, towns with rusted booms
Peer at the chromed main drag.

I trudged away over washed-out gullies,
Head down like a vanished buffalo;
A wind stirred out of the prairie,
The forever frontier wind tugged at my steps,
Suddenly I sang, I hiked through precious mud,
Past thousands of sunflowers bent fresh to the sun.

Clark Street, Chicago

The Street skids on its wrinkled face,
No mudpacks do it any good,
There's no beauty to restore,
Not in its hawking throat,
Nor in its limp skin of stagger,
Nor in that reddened eye of Law
Glaring above the paddy-wagon—
By mustached posters of stripteasers
I retch the bile that chokes me,
"Get it over with, Clark Street, die!"

But voices bud from weedy men;
Late at night, cocky with a dime,
Some free and easy ask for coffee.
On cracked lips of building rows
Dawn lights peaceful cigarettes—

Hands in pocket, Clark Street,
I pace by your lame lurch;
I sit by dirty cots of cafes,
Untrained to be a nurse,
And pity also cops and preachers,
The fists and ignorant fingers
That gouge your sores, and mine.

Washington Square, Chicago, USA

I heard an old man crack jokes
(An old musket clicking,
Pioneer powder gone dead)
On a box at bughouse square,
The dean of all those who
Spoke at Free Speech Square —

On my left, an old worker
Smoldered with ancient glow
Remembering Big Bill roar
On yellow-ugly Butte plateau —

On my right a jeweled girl
Laughed, "They really dare,
They really rave
Here at Washington Square."

Prepping for Europe,
A busload of tourist-gawk;
"The stupid government
Lets the damn Reds talk —"
"A young man ascends the box,
A Christian proud of Christ,
He deplores that the world
Keeps hunger, hate, and lice —
The next loves the freedom here,
And orating from his lair
To this hundred from the millions,
Eats on nickels from the Square.

O patch of sidewalk, grass, and queers,
Showplace of the First Amendment,

How you deserve your jeers!
A place of old men's voices,
And young men's shouted choices,
(Men between have just enough to lose,
And too little hope for gain,
To speak belief in public shoes),
These speakers feed on coin crumbs,
Cheap zoo for tourists, slummers, bums,
Old workers, dreamers of zions,
Cheap zoo for the hundred
With tastes for more than lions!
Plot of legalized rant,
Tired hymn against the sky's red ramp—
Forty miles of steel find defiant
Three voices, a box, a corner lamp—

I spit on the dirty sidewalk,
I vomit glare on the sooty leaves and talk;
When what I love turns furtive crook,
I want to kill the wriggle that's got me shook;
Die, you vulgar wriggle on the hook,
You Free Speech Square.

Hellas

Give it to me straight
About those snobby Greeks!
Your rant's aroused my mob . . .
Athenians jumped from Parnassus?
Athenians flung life away
Like a handfull of dirt?
What filthy convention joke then,
Those white columns to the sun?

I hear Baccantes scream,
I see the crush of crimson grapes,
I sit in the delphic clearing,
Stunned by the two-edged answer.

The Trucker

Raw ramming muscle.
Surge of push.
Strain of pull,
Bicep unfurled,
He snorted like a bull.

Catechism Offered To A Bartender

Time's a screwed-up sperm,
The moon a frozen rock,
And space a shaft with no way out;
I drink the night away.

Time was a brown-eyed girl,
The moon a dare to kiss,
And space a convenient orchard;
I drank the night away.

Time will run out of time,
Moon will leave the earth,
And space swell too large for any speck;
I'll drink the night away.

Walking Toward 72nd Street

In all that bulk of night and walls
I saw only three things shine—
The great white planet
His golden head
And your awakened eyes.

The untwinkling planet
Turned my heart as still as space,
His peroxide hair
Stirred me to a useless tear,
And your grave glance
Bent me like a laden bough.

I do not know
How so few things
Can make a world—
I know only three things shone
From all that bulk of night and walls—
The cold white light, his self-shorn head,
Your lustrous eyes.

All My Shadows

Perplexed by years and distance,
The infinite intersections,
Traveler lost from the start,
Beguiled by dreams gilding
My days with pastel plasters,
I, even if finely carved,
Will culminate at best a puppet
Flapped by poets struggling
To amuse pert new faces
To gain some small renown.

But flippantly sung
Or apparently forgot,
All my shadows,
And all of yours,
Will barnacle this ship.

The Parting

I sit alone in the public garden.
Not so long ago,
Hiking over grey pastures,
Through whitening cornstalks,
Or viewing the dirt-laden river
Roll slowly over cold sand,
We laughed with unconscious trust;
The sun, deflecting palely
Through soaked-cotton clouds,
Down gnarled grape vines,
On to peeling barns,
Fell chastely on us
Whose hearts sang,
Strolling windcombed grass.

Today white colonnades
Built misty-topped brights,
But elms arched a touchless symmetry
Around fingers of my thought;
And in this translucent twilight,
That interfuses me with night,
A single thrush calls for a long while
From high branches
Darkening an odorous honeysuckle.

More Central Than The Sun

That the moon would vanish,
And the stars,
And night at least bring rest!
No, not the moist night
When touch and sound and smell,
Lavish gamblers
Wagering blood and sperm
More prodigally than gold,
Outwit the eye's police!

My friend
Have more wine.
Down through clearest water
We see rocks shift and sway,
Through clearest sky
Sun is scattered blue;
And I have no hope
My words can be exact
When what they refract's
More central than the sun—
Thus I, whose path is language,
Will eagerly trace for you
A curious curve,
Most nearly elliptic,
That's now close, now far,
From what designs my days.
I've seen women cry,
More beautiful than birds,
Slashing as knives;
I've seen women cry
Like the salt sea in storm,
Like mossy wrecks
Becalmed and beached

Where long lianas
Clutched them greener yet.
I've seen myself nearly as brave
As in my dreams,
And nearly as coward
As in my fears,
And who am I?
The narrowing distance
Between hare and runner,
Slip in the crystal,
Dye not fast to the fabric,
The edge where love cuts hate,
And who am I?

I've seen men embrace
Stronger than granite,
Briefer than butterflies;
Men shift and sway
Scattering blue
With gestures of sun;
Men storm clouds and cannon
With equal preparation!
We wax and wax our chromium dreams,
Somehow they rust like other people's—
Yet, once, spume on oily waves
A hundred feet from a New York beach,
I mingled with sea and sky,
Completely as the ending of desire.
My friend,
Our wine is gone;
Dawn is waiting in the east
Like a weary wife,
Despair lids your eyes,
A hangover to come,

And I failed to make fireworks for you,
Moons of shall and stars of shan't—

But tomorrow or the next day
We will meet again,
Refracting in our words,
Swaying in our emotions,
Things more central than the sun,
More bottom than the rocks.

By the River of Dreams

The pines and mountains in that clear air Cezanne
The houses also French
The faintest violet reminded of the latitude
And only the Tet firecrackers' rattle
Recalled the threat of carbines:
In late morning, coffee and log fire
Drove off the chill when we emerged from blankets;
Beside the cool shadows sun lay down in warm sand
We stared at each other, incurious orchids,
We had known our common earth
We told our dreams
Forests, dark, light, intermingling,
A laugh, tears, silence,
Streaming embroidery of our past,
Touches, turning towards, turning aways,
Hopes, doubts, and calculations,
I jotted these notes
While you lined your eyes with green
On the screened small veranda;
I stopped to brush your hair.

Appetite

The step after step brought us
to the river
past the sandbags past the barbed wire
past the mountain ridge
past the moon past the stars
I stare, you ask
do you want cocoa and cake
Not when I face the night.

To L.E. On Leaving

I have loved you Lena
in such a way
that one year past
I would have jeered myself for fool
sneered what did you achieve
six kisses or were they only five
now I hunt rarer game
trophies of different kind
and this my love
whether you come to Nairobi or no
we bagged at El-Qurnah.

Hi

Sprinkled absently nowhere
                with absolute nothing
slammed on the brakes
crashed through the windshield
and somersaulted to enlightenment
under the gigantic dual tires
                of a superhighway truck
and with the hot asphalt
soaked up the furnaceous sun,
winking a red stop,
grinning a green go.

Autumn

Months of death!
At last laid fallow,
I escape my own history,
The urgent claims
Harvested again and again
Until my soil, worn-out,
Made ultimate protest of weeds.
I shall rest through ice and grass
Through perhaps the next and next,
But some soon spring,
I'll plant a better grain.

Zambezi

Kings and Queens in suburbs
powerless and periphery checkmate
while elephants trunk to tail
roar fearfully crossing Zambezi
of city exhaust and executions
even here by the orange thick viper
beneath the thick orange moon
I tongue the smokestacks
of Bulawayo forms and shapes of logic
crocodiles deposit screaming freight
the air shudders and sweats dust
rocks quake on iron jelly
drums and fires
upon mountain nights
drive to destruction
game the heart desires

Mombasa

The white woman with crossed hands
decorates the car,
her breasts packed carefully, fat oiled fish.

Ghosts of mangoes drip orange
through creaking fronds
and it shines down the sand
to bloody the sea.

I drank from ten shilling love
nightly in the roof house rooms
spume
yes, but the waves recur.

Mud

You said, Zoltan,
A poem has to stick around
long enough to show it means business—
three lines are a bitch's smile
in a drawing room—
The inelegance has to show—
The poet's got to get stuck
that's sticking around
even stuck in the mud
but black sucking water-soaked gumbo
stuck sucking yucking muck
real mud you can squeeze out of your fist
and feel it squirting out
not mud that's just gonna make dirt
and produce the old waving red-white-and blue wheat
but mud that'll dry, pack, crack, hardpan,
and you have to plow and plow
be cunning with struggle with then Johnson grass—
Then you know he's really stuck around,
Right Zoltan?

Believe Me

Would you believe the unbelievable
if it happened right in front of you?
I don't believe it
not till I see you believe
right in front of me.

Dance

I would like to say
DANCE
and like that easy, man,
with the cheapest magic
groove you in delight
but even DANCE DANCE DANCE
won't do it
oh it's not easy
dance you words
dance   dance dance
hey go words go   dance
dance   dance
            dance   dance
                         DANCE

Take-Off from Saigon

Shoppers flapped across the reach of noon,
Rusted jokes leaned on receivers,
Lazy sluts razzled violence from the hoist crowd,
Cupboard kin brayed their pots and pans,
We rolled into the sand of worn-out years,
Nicked and baling-wired machines,
Sea-girls slickered the lighthouse men
Roar and rant
I laugh and cry
And quickly trade this universe.

Tangier Talk

Crocodiles sleep like bones
Sun spider webs the swamps
Sidereal time eclipses moon
Defeat streams mucous flags
Genius abandons barricades
In streets abandoned to machines
Grey snows fall on white confetti
Big ones ground to little ones
One palm tree a park
And three talk of this in Tangier
Where oranges sell cheap Arabs
And everyone as everywhere
Dreams yesterday's gold.

January 1, 1964

Everybody drunk
including straw mats
or stoned someway
and thrown to winds
as sooner later
everybody blown
including straw mats
so fly now fly high.

Love the Moon

Night Night Night
Is Day in China
Day Day Day is night in China
Lounge and scrounge on venture
Columbus and not Ohio
On the road reach sonorous gongs
For past American wrongs
Nor heed my cheap queen's chains
Because she sees bedraggled Indians
And dungeons me
As I did a shamanic chief
Night Night Night
Is Night Everywhere Night
And Thank God
For Day's a Drag
Forget contour lines
And bottom lines
And Love the Moon
The Night devours
And I disappear
To return only on special occasions.

Abstracting

I

Dark flood
Toes dabble
Flotsam surf
Cave flee to
Sun huddle
Hug the biggest lie

II

Dark
dabble
flotsam
flee
huddle
lie

III

Dark
flotsam
lie

IV

Flotsam Flotsam Flotsam

December in Tangier

Rain rain
Again
Again
Again
Rain rain
Strokes croaks
Lowers pours
Wet flit
Pet wit
Crazy
Lazy
Rain rain
No sun
Some fun
Rain rain
Maleeka

Maleeka

Bird of the night
Girl of the cafe
Brown legs of harvest and moon
No's and Yes's of four languages
Strong breasts pushed out to kiss
Of the quiet tight writhe
Of quick affront
Of sixteen year childishness
Maleeka
Gliding to me in the dark
Serpent of the moment's wisdom.

Fort Roseberry, Zambia

Why shouldn't I be sitting here on my can
My can of chicken Johnny Meeser gave me
Steve, I don't know his last name
Promised me dinner at sundown
If no ride came.
About three hundred miles down
The dusty road lies Chitimukulu
Where I hope to dance
And drink Chipumu beer
And talk with the Chief
I'll get there sometime
The shadows lengthen
"A long journey, bwana"
No longer than anyone else's I reckon
Too damn short.

Victoria Falls

Last night and today
basaltic, green, and foam-sprayed
smoke-that-thunders
I turned to you more often
than to a new smooth girl
after a month's safari.

City

Steel and canned music
Nairobi and New York
Books
Sex for money and drinks
Fear of murder
Fear of hope
Desperate talk over tea or coffee.

Equilibrating

When one is too content for written words
But botches up at drawing
And for several reasons
Can't continue talking through the night
Under the intimate blankets
There's nothing much left to do
But stand
Make some hopefully not too pat a gesture
Leave
Stride a bit in stars and breeze
Universe provides just the proper balance.

Pathless Voyage

And why should you respond?
Why should wind blow
Oh if the two ways were the same!
I could journey to that lati- longi-tude
Across dimensionless oceans
Wait out dry seasons
Knowing rain would come
But who or what predict a yes
Or yes appearing what further yesses
No, in these adventures
There're no grids, no proved or provable charts
Only hope, meditation, doubt,
Sustaining labor keeping shipshape,
And signals from receding shores.

Past the Word

I frankly detest this word love
    grimed
    hoboken rusted and rundown
    ghost town
    slattern pattern
    leaf skeleton
    flowered and now rotted seed
    of provencal broken-off coitus
    ecstasy dreams from half-yes
    one live coal
    in embers of a black death world
    much better, wordless,
you kissed me lingering lazy back
    in the bombed-out ruins of rumors,
when your hand encountered the chill barbed wire
you reached for me with the other,
you hunkered down and smoked your cigarette,
we told each other of the ironic past
where we learned at least to laugh and cry,
and then we bounded up, ran down night gravel,
irrationally chuckled among the flares,
turned in, and woke for show and work.

Aphorisms

Aphorisms

Life is the creative imagination of the dead.

Death is the experience we all know the most about while claiming we know nothing about it.

Society consists of the people we fear; solitude of the people we love.

How many have stopped thinking because they could not bear being so ashamed of those around them?

Emotion is fire looking for dry grass and drier wind; put it to work in the alchemical furnaces.

Luck is taking up the attitude of opportunity in a world built on catastrophe.

Truth strikes a new spot each time it hits: No one becomes "used to it".

Investigating the forbidden is irresistible since we are well aware that the deformed nature of forbidders leads them to unerringly include the best as well as a few of the obviously worst in their lists of verboten.

Freedom never tells what is behind the door that it allows us to open; the unprepared relax in exultation and are often devoured on the spot.

Generosity gives others their due, without demanding one's own.

Humility gives its own due, without demanding any recognition from others; an effective manner of operating in a world of vanity and pride.

Humiliation is the cheap price by which a saint hopes to purchase immortality.

Virtues are rational when their advantages can be calculated by mathematicians of the spirit.

Domestic politics is the extension of war by means of the police.

Crime is how the market outwits the monopolists.

War is the method by which human primates send off the young and strong from the old bull's territory.

College education is the method by which human primates beat up the young and strong who stay around the old bull's territory.

The young and strong learn by imitation and grow themselves up to treat the next young and strong just the way they were treated, that is, repress them for as long as possible.

Jobs are the cleverest way to capture a higher mammal ever devised.

A bibliography proves that one has not been guilty of an independent thought.

Theatre lets the secret out, that it all depends on the actor, the audience, the script, the director, the lighting, the stage set, the house, and the time of year, week and day, and above all, that, no matter what, the show must go on.

Poetry conceals the secret by a metaphor, and wants to keep the secret a secret, convinced that direct truth is too much for humans and a direct lie too little.

Science knows that the more it knows, the more it knows that it does not know, hence, is the best home since 1700 for genuine mystics.

Truth, even a small part of it, can't stand the exposure of longer than a single sentence, or else it pales.

Desire, without capacity and skill, is the greatest disaster that can strike a man.

Satire is the first psychological step above revenge.

"The people" are the stock-in-trade of the rhetoricians, and the stock is always marked On Sale.

The rhetorician can convince a human to do something he never thought about before, and will shudder at later.

Sickness is the body's meditation on death.

Poverty is the major proof of the powers of the magic of money.

The street waits for people to fall from the skyscraper.

Mathematics is insight for the contemplative, weapon for the rulers, and criminal for the poor to possess beyond enough to count their bills to the last penny.

Experience is what we can take from the universe without a protest.

Understanding is what we can digest from experience but nostalgia will always protest.

Experience disappears when we talk about it, and is forgotten when we don't talk about it.

Belief is the morphine of the emotions; dogmatic belief is crack for the passions.

Gossip is the inflation of psychology; it takes a lot to buy a little insight.

Scholars are the real estate brokers of history.

History will always be the best-selling popular novel that's also the classic of tomorrow.

We do anything to avoid trying for the impossible; however, that ordeal's our only chance to rescue the possible.

Our potential is wasted if we try to actualize less than four aspects at once, as the great pyramid tells us.

Step by step, the ziggurat admonishes us; I love these simple messages written so big that the most near-sighted can see them, and with such blank pages that anyone can write his novel on them.

Poetry is the form of literature that adopted the stop exercise to end each line.

Money is super magic: black money can be laundered into white money by the stroke of a pen, white money into black by a single purchase.

When money loses its magic, and its value drops, new magicians must draw a different circle and pronounce new names; a new party comes to power, announces the press.

When naked, alone, unseen and unsurprisable, at night, one can weigh the chains of society by watching the poverty and lack of invention of one's movements.

Our skin protects us far better than any of our thoughts and attitudes: who knows where their allegiance lies, from whom they were sent, and to whom they are sending their prepared signals?

No one has seriously dreamed of being read a million years from now, much less written for such an audience, yet we know that a million years is only a wink in evolutionary time.

How can we any longer pay sustained attention to anyone so subjective as not to be writing for a reader also in the next species or two?

We know the size and shape of the earth, even the galaxy, but not of our passion, our mood, our philosophy, our sensation, our future; the pettiness of our inner geographers keeps explorers from launching anything larger than rowboats.

Suppose the inner geography were as complex and far-reaching as the outer geography? Supposing one's passion were to be explored by a crew with the same thoroughness and energy as a coral reef, one's thought like a biosphere?

A real teacher is someone resourceful enough to make new discoveries.

A real student is someone resilient enough to let himself be discovered.

Sleep was considered the highest state by the ancients because it combines the best of death and life: it's both painless and regenerative.

Friendship is the most exciting gamble: reinforcement or betrayal?

Enmity is the most rigorous training: the enemy plans to destroy you through your weaknesses and the ferocity of his attack makes it impossible for you to cover them up and gives but little time to repair them.

Love is war games of the spirit.

I dare say only the first sentence of each message.

A mastery of at least two options on each of at least twelve levels gives one a fighting chance.

We have a machine, an apparatus, and a utility; but we have to make the tools to adjust them and learn the mission rules to operate them.

Life is something that the oldest live too short a while to know much about, but if we take it as a gift it makes our future.

An argument is the ultimate test of good will toward our own digestion.

Silence, laughter, and rhythm are three irrefutable expressions.

An actor always holds something in reserve.

Stalk and study those who hunt you if you can't get out of their ecosystem; then change your behavior to a species not on their food chain, migrate, or begin to hunt the hunter.

Words move like an exponentially increasing virus throughout society until they have killed the originating insight. The way to kill the virus is not to speak a word without a fresh specific reference to an observed and visualized sensation, emotion or thought.

The word virus is evolved into symbiosis only by making sure that the cell of experience to which it applies is large and healthy enough to support both beings.

Plutarch's Lives are a source-book of possibilities for character.

Magic transformed into money. Religion to advertising. Science to politics. Superstition . . . remained superstition.

Sex touches our deepest being. Eros touches the other's deepest being.

If the great thoughts of death, infinity, delight, and the good are not integrated into my thinking, I must think what recourse the small thoughts of life, limitation, sorrow, and the bad.

The Hindu Rasikas of drama insisted that the moods of horror, the odious, and the furious were as important as the marvelous, the transcendent and the erotic; then the heroic, poignant, and comic could grow to their full stature, equal with the mighty primal six.

There is an agony that exists greater than being defenseless under a savage attack; when one can't defend one's friends and beloveds from being included in that savage attack upon oneself.

We are all attacked by time, by space, by energies, by things, by enemies, and by the uncomprehending, who neither know, nor feel, nor sense, what they are doing, as ants are crushed by boots who never sense anything between themselves and the concrete.

It, therefore, behooves us to arm ourselves at many levels and in many ways: stealth, invisibility, mirrors, inebriants, poisons, decisiveness, obfuscations, procrastinations, rhetoric, logic, forethought, intuition, vigilance, shrewdness, quickness, randomness, camouflage, transformations, transfers, breakdowns, negotiations, retreats, redoubts, strategies, tactics, history, alertness, courage and cowardice, truth and lies, sanity and madness, celebration and mourning, laughter and tears.

Let sleeping dogs lie, otherwise they may bound up, follow you, and eat you out of house and home besides digging up the garden, while barking the neighbors into hating you.

If the shoe fits, wear it unless you can go barefooted.

Death and taxes are unavoidable for any citizen of any state.

One man's accident is another man's luck and yet another man's opportunity.

Create? Yes, then run for your life.

I must not only know but understand that the language operating my cells is as old/young as those operating the live oak, the catfish, the rattlesnake, the golden eagle, the gila monster, the dragonfly, and the buffalo grass.

The planet is formed from concentrated debris from exploded stars, my body from concentrated debris from ransacked ecosystems, my book from concentrated debris from refuted volumes.

Explosions, ransacking, refutations generate energy to create new components from which forms yet greater with potentiality can emerge.

There are many advantages to living long and healthily, not least that contemplation and reflection need time also to attain to an approximation of disillusioned impartial judgement of motives and probable consequences underlying behavioral sequences of animals, humans, and archetypes, so contorted, twisted, hidden, duplicitous, involved, knotted, and full of potential can these behaviors be, not to speak of the satisfaction and advantages in outliving your enemies.

On leaving, sighs of relief counterpoint sighs of regret, and on arrival, smiles of apprehension segue with smiles of anticipation.

Courtesy is a tribute one pays to oneself; if generous, one has enough for others as well; no gift is better received.

Some pass through the mirror and it becomes a window; others look back and see a blank surface; they remain in one world albeit a different one.

For the arche gods and goddesses to live, we must give them a good deal of our life and from the best of our attention; few people care for the investment today in their pursuit for immediate stimuli, so the sacrifice market has never been better; the powers are hungry.

Mean and dangerous men say, I sold out my dreams so, in revenge, I will kill yours; the mean-spirited have found three ideal palaces from which to issue their decrees of mental torture and execution: the media, the university, and the government.

If you want to lose a finger, lift it to stop someone from heading toward a disaster glowing with glamour from the derailed sex energy of denials, splittings and projections; if you want to lose more, lift your hand and arm; if you want to lose your neck, lift your voice to speak.

Conjugations of the logos:
I talk to evacuate the brain; I converse for amusement and learning; I say to get a point across; I lecture to transmit information and/or inspiration; I speak to transmit my stand; I dialogue to build a scenario; I interject to keep things going or to stop them; I fall silent to radiate, emanate, concentrate, or listen when someone else emits the living word; I act when I have heard.

The universe is authored by a repertory playwright who keeps adding new plays, stage managed by a master physico-chemist, directed by an expert evolutionist with the dangerous tools of variation and selection, produced by the synergetic action of us, them, and those, each center of experience, will-he, nill-he, is perforce an actor on the omni-reflecting non-simultaneous stage of time-space, energy, matter, life, intelligence, and dreams, whether one learns to act, allows oneself to be typecast, or plays an extra in the crowd.

There's no point finding your own voice if you have nothing of your own to say with it.

With so many theories of immortality: physico-chemical, genetic, mimetic, remembrance, historic, literary, soul, spiritual, conscious, reincarnational, eternal, anyone really interested in accomplishing the feat would have to master a number of disciplines, each of which could require a lifetime, none of which has ever been proven to work. With so many facts of mortality: body, emotional, intellectual, sensual, sexual, societal and species, no one has ever worked out the theory of death. No one ever flew until gravitational fact showed that the airplane would always fall toward the center of the earth with a force equal to its mass times 32 feet per second, per second. Then theory could calculate the power and design needed to fly.

Promises

The many who break their word must not make us underrate keeping our word. Those who break their word, we can cease dealing with in any essential way and so their damage ability is limited. Those who do keep their word, we can deal with for the years of whatever task we share; as for keeping one's own word, we must deal with ourselves for at least the rest of our lives.

Short Stories

The Dead Indian Mounds

Unafraid, he stared as close to the sun shinier than tin as his eyes could bear. Never in his seven years had the light-flecked blue deepened so; it slowly revolved, pricking his eyes with tiny brilliant needles. Dizzy, exalted, he stumbled just before he could complete an emotion luring and decisive.

He felt charged with daring, with impatient energy; his mother, leading him and his small brother home from their picnic in the woods, seemed intolerably cautious. He bowed his head and galloped past her and around a bend in the path.

Peering into shadows intertwined with light, he pretended Indian stealth, cleverly side-stepped dry twigs, crouched low when he rustled a leaf, crept ever closer to an unsuspecting enemy.

"Ned, you come back here," his mother cried nasally.

His scouting party shattered on thoughts of her thin hardness, her tight mouth, darting eyes, her hands, small freckles scattered between blue upraised veins, gestures instinct with freezing derision. Blurred with resentment, suffocated from his joy, he had to escape.

"I'm going to take a shortcut," he yelled.

"Now you be careful. You better come on back!"

"I'll beat you to the road, Momma!" Skulking through the stunted oaks, avoiding ambushes, he soon evaded his mother's reproaching image, and the peculiar, fluttering liveliness of the day returned. Seeing the glint of hovering and darting wings, he pursued a butterfly from light to shadow before it escaped.

Sand spushed beneath his feet. Gnarled and twisted, the scrub oak, porcupined with twigs, oppressed him with the motionless struggles of their shapes. Only the hot, cricking locusts splashed sound into the humid silence of the Oklahoma summer.

Suddenly, bursting open in front of him, the air seemed to hum with a golden light. His breaths seemed taut as a murmuring string. Right at his feet a cliff dropped sheerly down, down to the valley which he knew held the three mounds with dead Indians inside.

The trail had nearly disappeared; it wound below the edge of the cliff only a foot in width, but still he wanted to follow it like a pioneer even though the rock looked fractured and loose. This time, in this vibrant haze of air that hung over the valley, he would find the rest of that emotion he had come so close to finishing while staring into the blue at the edge of the sun. Putting his back to the cliff, he edged rapidly sideways a hundred feet before coming to a gap.

It was about four feet across the gap, and there was a bush growing out of the rocks that he could swing across on, but still he felt a thrill of fear. He shouldn't have come so far by himself. He wanted to go back. He could say, "Momma, the trail ended."

But he imagined her scornful eyes, she would know he was lying. He could not stand up to her with a lie; she would find out. He would have to stand in front of her, eyes down, neck burning, telling all that he was ashamed of . . .

Overborne, desperate with intensity that had steadily built up inside him, he grabbed hold of the bush and swung himself over the gap almost before he knew what he was doing. He was breathing hard, and still holding with one hand to the bush, but he took his time to enjoy his new view and self-prestige.

For the first time he looked straight down to the bottom of the valley, green, thick and lush with grass that shared the same mysterious liveliness that seemed to fill the air and oaks. And just to this right were the three Indian mounds, their grass greener, thicker, softer, more inviting, yes, just as he had felt drawn up into a slowly revolving vortex of blue now he felt drawn down upon those mounds.

The blood in his arm clutching the bush constricted with faintness, yet never had he breathed such sweet and murmuring air, seen grass so green and soft. And the thought came glinting out of the shadows like the butterfly he had chased. Surely he would not be harmed if he jumped.

Was this the emotion he had sought all that lively sun-flecked day when he had but to look at an object to feel its very rhythms? The temptation murmured more hazily golden than the air. But his heart caved away, and he heard himself panting. How terrible the world must be if a jump to such green grass killed him!

The harsh cawing of a crow startled him. He looked upward at the bird blackly flapping its way across the valley.

He knew the crow was a warning, and still he wanted to jump; the thought of possible death, fearful as it was, made the desire seem more tender and attractive than before.

The crow cawed harshly in his memory. He would be killed. And as his certainly grew, his fear grew and his disgust. Could not Peter have walked on water if he had perfect faith?

Nonetheless he could not move, staring down, entranced by the grass below, now seeing the same light-flecks in it that had been in the blue. Something happen, he cried to himself, something happen; he was no longer master of himself, the forces that made him move were annihilating his mind.

Trembling uncontrollable, his knees crumpled. Gratefully, he made himself edge back against the rock, sweat greasy on his forehead, his heart empty with fear.

The green softness below now seemed to beckon him in shameless evil, "You will never know unless you jump and find out. You are too much of a coward ever to know. Jump and find out."

He saw no more; thankfully, he felt himself submerged in a preserving panic, his hands wetly clawed at the bush, and he swung himself once more over the gap, thudding against the rocky ledge. Cut and bloody, he crawled all the way to the top in terror, gasping for breath in the upper part of his lungs, his stomach flattened against his spine.

Reaching the top, he gathered his strength and ran and fell and fell and ran, careless of stinging twigs, seeing nothing but shadowy sand alternating with light gold sand. Steam seemed to explode from a valve. "Rattler!" he thought. A cottontail started up like a shotgun blast at his feet.

"Momma, Momma!" His fright wrenched loose from deep down as her sharp face and thin mouth came into focus, her broad and substantial skirt.

"I could have killed myself. I almost killed myself. I wanted to jump and find out." His arms tightened humbly around her legs.

Suddenly remembering her old derision, he looked up at her through the burn of his tears. But no scorn was in her eyes; she seemed puzzled, even fearful herself, though her hand was patting his shoulder, steadily, intensely, like the time he cut his foot so badly. She did not understand.

Trudging on home ahead of his mother and little brother, he hung his head, looking minutely and unseeing at the small rocks in the path. From where came this teeter of life and death? The mounds full of the long dead Indians grew tumultuous with riddles. And, very calm now, recollecting every detail of his journey, he became almost frightened of himself.

The Monkey

The four messengers sat on the bench and watched the game. They each wore clean short khaki pants, short-sleeved khaki skirts, black shoes with black knee-length hose, and khaki felt hats with one side pinned up and a red band around the brim. Two men sat on the ground on one side of the game board and one man lay on the ground on the other side. All of the men were in the shade of the village's big mango tree and there was still a lot of shade left over even at midday. They had been playing the game since the sun cleared the tops of the thatched huts a hundred feet east of them. The game board had been carved out of a solid piece of hard wood. Instead of squares, it had scooped-out pockets. The men playing deftly distributed and redistributed small white and black stones.

A very small, but very wizened grey monkey watched the men sitting on the bench and the men sprawled on the ground. The monkey had not sat there all morning, however. He had scampered away several times, once hanging on a thorn tree across the clearing and jabbering at the men. Two of the men had risen and walked over to look at him then. Two girls, each with a gasoline can full of water perched on the folded cloth on her head, had stopped to look at the monkey first. When the girls stopped joking and moved on, the men left the monkey and returned to their bench.

Once one of the messengers yelled and a little girl emerged from one of the huts a minute later. She brought him a cigarette. One of the players brought up a box of matches from his pocket. The lit cigarette was passed around to everyone.

The monkey had taken a short nap, but on waking up he moved very close to the men. Finally he walked around between them, trailing his tail. Most of them laughed, but one messenger waved the back of his hand toward the monkey.

The monkey drew himself up and stared at the man.

The man hit the monkey lightly. The monkey turned rigid and, baring its teeth, spit and hissed at the man.

"You don't do that to me, monkey!" The man smashed the monkey down with his hand. The monkey did not roll away, but started to raise itself again. The man smashed the monkey as hard as he could with his fist. Blood spurted. The monkey, rolling away, barely missed being crushed by a stamping foot.

The game had stopped. The men stared first at the bleeding monkey, standing, facing the men from about ten feet away, and then at the man who hit the monkey. The man who had hit the monkey made two attempts to rise, but each time sat right down again. His arm flailed at the monkey like the reflexes of a dying animal and then subsided. There was a moment's silence and all the men stared at the monkey.

The monkey stopped facing the men. Its attention focused on the blood streaming along its arm. Suddenly the monkey bent its head and licked at the blood. A pleased expression flashed on its face. The monkey greedily licked all the blood off its arm, and then reached up to wipe the blood from its forehead, and then to lick that blood from its fingers.

The men started laughing. Finally two or three of them were roaring and imitating the monkey's licking its blood. The man who hit the monkey finally lost the anger on his face. One of the men on the ground reached toward the game board and redistributed the stones again. The messengers' attention shifted back to the game.

The monkey, with a rapt observant expression, kept licking away, at slightly different accumulations, his slowly appearing blood.

One Evening

"Timber-r-r!" Mike yelled and the thirty-foot long two-by-twelve beam, uprooted by three blows of his crowbar, slid off the naked roof.

Mike grinned at the lean shirtless youngster straddling a rafter prying up the next board. "Here we go, Ben, next!" He strode down the roof pausing only to yank gigantic pulls against the twelve-penny nails holding down the end, the middle, and the far end of each board.

"Timber-r-r!" Each board took bare seconds.

The men below, nail-pullers and haulers, stopped their labor momentarily to laugh and marvel at Mike, off again on one of his sprees of physical skill and prowess. They laughed admiringly even though they would have to sweat to keep up with him.

Another pair were working the roof, but they, too, stopped to watch Mike and his helper fall to for a few minutes. "Timber-r-r!"

They left work early that Saturday afternoon. Ben parted from Mike with a long handshake and walked out of town down a narrow dusty street.

He felt his muscles loose and hard after working all winter and he began jogging when the road dwindled to two ruts ruled off between pastures. His nostrils dilated with the air, sweet from blowing softly over the late March wheat and oats and alfalfa, all freshly green with spring, the soil still a rich dark from the winter rains, the wind-blown and white parched dust of August still far off. The low hills around the valley undulated a deep cool blue against the nuzzling blue of the sky and a red-winged blackbird tweeted.

He jogged off the road into a grove of widely spaced pecan trees and then walked on more leisurely. He knew a creek on the other side of the grove.

Sunlight formed golden pools between the well-spaced stately pecan trees. The shadowed ground looked cold. Knock-knock-knock. A woodpecker startled his revery which was turning into the curious mysteries of light and dark and pecan groves, hollowing out strange vistas almost beyond thought and emotion.

He spread two rusty strands of barbed wire and straightened up among the tangled undergrowth of crowded oaks and cottonwoods. Old trunks and branches lay rotting on the damp life-filled ground, steamy with the first warm sun, and ropy vines dangled limply from the oaks.

A crow sailed slowly and blackly from a high cottonwood limb and he could not turn his eye until it silently flapped out of sight. Fancies and images and words almost thoughts poured into his mind ever more as he pursued his way.

They fell slowly into his mind, and the least seemed profound, and yet they were confused and then he noticed he did not see the sun. A dusky gold interfused down from the tops of the trees but the woods were almost dark. It seemed to him that he saw a long path, thorny and seldom used, over which some toiled a silent way, and where a deep sadness pervaded all things. He poked his toe slowly through the rotted bark of a fallen cottonwood, and then he looked up at the tallest cottonwood which stood very tall and firm and whose leaves murmured like a stream in the breeze.

Then he came upon the creek and he sat down on the sheared bank and looked down on the shallow water sparkling over white sand. Here and there long shadows fell across the creek.

He sat there some time unconscious of all things except the ceaseless flow of water. Minute after minute it continued, it simply continued without regard to minutes, always clear, always making clear bubbling sounds, always hurrying down to the river which would take it to the sea. Its motion, always forward, possessed his mind and he watched greedily small twigs borne down its course until they lodged against a sandbank or disappeared from sight.

Then the top of the woods suffused with dusky reddish gold. He started up and raced along the bank of the creek toward the river. He stumbled through underbrush, jumped small eroded gullies, and plunged into a large oatfield. The oats came above his knees; they were blue green. Insects called and shirred in the tall grass. Tears came to his eyes from the running and he strained to see.

Then the river bank, and he stopped in a great silence. The tiny creek below him ran sparkling gold into the dark river while directly across jutted a large sandbank around which the powerful current flowed.

On up the sandbank began a thick woods, now all dark except for a reddish gold on the tops of the very tallest trees, and this reddish golden light did not seem to come from the trees but seemed to envelop them and blot out their individual characteristics.

And suddenly he was not conscious of existence, only perhaps of a deep feeling of joy, not to shout or caper, but all the same a joy, not his, which not only filled but threatened to burst forth from him and envelop him for it seemed like the golden light that bloomed around the treetops.

And then he watched the light fade slowly down to a faint red line where he could see parts of the horizon through the woods, then finally the broken red line vanished. He stayed there until the last translucence vanished from the sky and night had ascended and descended everywhere, and until the stars and dark hollow rushing of the river dominated everything.

Then he walked slowly back to town where he would have a late supper of beans and ham and rejoin the crew.

Guerrilla War in VietNam

The man piled up at the bar door in planes and cubes, a Grenade, Hand, Fragmentation, ready to explode.

He joggled, safety on, to street level, strode past the squatting wrinkle-faced seller of smooth sliced papaya, and rigidly left-turned. Toward me his jaw jutted steel blue prickles.

"This street's not big enough for both of us."

"I said this street's not big enough for you and me."

"Because I say it's not."

"Because I don't like your looks."

"Mister, I'm looking for trouble and when I saw you I knew I found it."

"When I beat a man up, he's beaten like he's never been beaten."

"Because it pleases me."

"Alright. I want some action. They won't send me to the action. So I booze here looking for action."

"Yeah. I drank twenty-eight beers one sitting. Something, huh?"

Below checkered Bermudas, his square knees and slablike calves foundation-stoned him where he stood. His clenched fist measured my jaw. He was half-drunk. That small non-coordination would be my only chance. Except retreat.

So why did I eyeball to eyeball this ticking bomb? Like was it cool not to leave this spot of 15 piastre beer and 200 piastre girls?

He held me. My left knee shook, a leaf, but I'd just hiked hours lonely, restless, along glistening tidal flats, banked freighters smoldering under heavy stars I once more as in a thousand and thirteen before places seeking the secret that perhaps does not exist. At last, at last some action. I could not retreat.

"If you don't stop talking in ten seconds I'm going to break your jaw."

Meaning ten seconds or a minute? My exact response never entered memory, dead so quick the so quick.

But softly to the effect he could take all the street except the inches where I reassembled and the little air I carbonized. Perhaps he didn't want to hit a man who kept his hands down. Perhaps he had only wanted to make me interested. Perhaps, but one may read many books, travel around longitudes and latitudes, and still one's own behavior, not to lie of others', though examined, remains enigma.

"You only have two things I want — your beard and your words. The army won't let me grow the one and I quit the tenth grade."

He plucked out, aplomb, his pack of cigarettes and offered.

"I only drink."

"Okay, I'll buy you a drink."

He plunged off across the street to a bar mainly for officers. All the girls on that side were the graceful Ao Zai and long hair, on the other side slacks, short skirts and bouffant hair. But officers and men garnered as often the same bad luck.

He turned on his stool to face me. I flipped after a second's confrontation. Try looking at another man. Try how long. If you're like me, pretty soon you'll tap your fingers, cross your legs, look at his shoes, if no one else is around you'll look at stains, a slab of sky, start swilling. Like when you tune in someone's wavelength there's buildup, the waves faster, the sounds shriller, finally it's pain and you turn the damn thing off.

Turned on his stool, he poked his bristler ever forward. It was like the side of a house falling down and inside a family screaming.

"I'd give this much of my dick to express myself."

He placed his thumb and index finger two inches apart. Maybe you got eight and can afford it, I thought.

"A man can be good at anything, but he can be great in only one thing."

He repeated himself.

"He can be great in only one thing."

I sat there like Greek before the delphic. Where did his sentences come from? Magazines, street corner bull, hand-me downs from atheist uncle, some origination of his own flashing electric clickers?

He'd finally landed his punch. Jack-of-all-master-of-no-trades me. Why hadn't I become a great pooh-bah or blah-blah?

"A man has to find that one thing he can be great at."

How many times I'd tilted this tournament. I knew all shocks of non-recognition. Yet I listened like a baby listens to rolling who-knows-what-they-mean mama papa speeches feeling must understand because it might be magic. What? What is one thing I can be great at?

"The thing I can do is fire weapons. At a hundred and twenty-five yards I can empty an M-14 into a space the size of my palm. There's only one thing each man can be great at."

"Firing weapons, out thinking the enemy that's what I'm great at. But since

I haven't really done it, how do I really know?"

How does one know? He's beating me up worse than with his fists, only deep I love this way beaten-up, physically no, no, a broken nose too permanent, only one body, but have a few thousands souls to spare, expandable, flay them again and again into the fray, meat hook each new faith on question. If they don't do it, how do you know? But there's a lot of things to do, and what if you pick wrong five times running, life's gone?

"We use to throw cards. Face down, we fight, face up, we didn't. Stupid, huh? But that's the way we did it when I was thirteen."

A tough one, alright. I saw him by the pool table on Halstead Street, cockier than the rattling street car, colder than the Lake Michigan wind, more hood than Stockyards stink, bending, stroking his cue, carefully rolled to check the deviation, lining up on veed thumb and finger, then follow-through breaking the rack wide-open with a blasting bust, transmuting his grin into swaggered one hand lean on table while at least three balls plunk plunk plunk. I saw the time he found out you don't feel pain when you hit the sidewalk during a fight, only later, and that if you've won, that stiff bruise's nothing to the burned-out peace surrounded and supported by respect and self-respect. And the time he found out he had to prove it again, and again.

"This Caribou bellied in with a hundred and fifty-five gigs, you know what I mean? I'm a leader. I took that ship over. I owned that ship for four and a half days and then they flew it away, you never own anything working with aircraft. You fix'em up and they fly 'em away. You don't ever own 'em."

"Have you ever seen a sergeant who was a leader? I'm an idolizer. All Americans are. I idolize my SP-6. He works all day on a prop and doesn't catch a speck of dirt. I worked a half-day once, from seven to twelve, and I didn't catch a speck, working with grease. My front buckle shiny as when I started and the back of my belt clean. I'm serious. A soldier should be clean."

"Yes," I said formal as a placard. He was beginning to maunder. How once I'd sought out each glint and dark on a banyan leaf! How I fled this faceless mob!

"There's that one word we don't know. You tell me this one word to help suffering. You tell me the one word to tell someone who's buddy's been killed. Who's been shafted by a Dear John letter. There isn't any word. I'd give anything to know that word. Only poets are happy. They come closer to knowing that word than anyone else."

I wanted to say yes, yes. I wanted to face again the delphic. The Dear John bit pissed me off. I couldn't picture it so suffering. Who wants a girl who doesn't love you? I didn't want to empathize. I wanted him to stir old fear, arouse awe by hurling brute words charged with lightning. He was lying. Suffering would be his being wounded, not a buddy's being killed, not his being killed because that's fine. Why didn't he admit he was afraid.

"I think I'd kill any man I saw smirking at the American flag, even another American."

"I think you might."

"You know, I could hate you all over again. I'm supposed to be a big tough motherfucker who never gives. Why am I talking?"

He stared at me but I saw I had disappeared. He swung around, slid off the stool, and bounced away. We'd've had to get drunk, or laid, or in a fight or all three if he'd stayed on.

Conversation

Except for the war, we might just as well have been sitting on bar stools back in his coal mining hometown in Kentucky. The beer was cheaper, more girls were hanging out at the bar and they lips were slightly fuller, their noses shorter, and they wouldn't freckle in the sun.

But there was the same expectant Saturday night air, the beer flowed down (no moonshine here), and the same need to talk about his trade, his wife, his hopes.

He was profane like every fighting soldier except General Lee. He happened to sit down by me and out here propinquity makes for quick reaction.

"I'll buy your next beer," he said. "You look new."

"Just got in today."

I confessed to a gutless feeling and started asking questions. Where was it safe to go? Was it true you couldn't go out of Saigon at night? And suchlike.

"Alright to go up the river to Cholon (Chinatown) long as you stay within a mile on this side of it and don't go too deep into Cholon. Nobody'll bother you here in the city.

I remembered the blasted-out windows on the fifth floor of the Caravelle Hotel down the street but stayed quiet.

"Only seventy-six days to go. My year's up then. A year's a long time when your wife's nineteen.

He, it turned out, was twenty-two. Finishing his third year in the paratroopers. "I know what you mean by gutless. Hell, I been too scared to move. They got me here." His finger moved alongside his side.

"They sent me to the Philippines. Officer was there I knew. Damn fine man. They put two clean bullet holes in him and they fizzed him up good in Saigon the same day. Looked clean as a whistle. But they sent him to the Philippines. They knowed the infections'd come. Sure enough the twenty-second day he swole up. Broke out everywhere."

My daddy was a master sergeant. I reckon he'd be proud of me now. I'm an E-5 and I reckon I'll make 6 this next year. I'm gonna put in for Special Services — that's fifty-four weeks you know, one year and two weeks. They want you trained. They got spit and polish, but I can make it. Learned how to make them old boots stand up and shine."

"Special Services was President Kennedy's own idea, I mean it was his baby. Yeah they're good. I want to tell you that Viet Cong is ee-leet, too, the ee-leet of the ee-leet, they're ever bit as good as the Special Services, maybe a little better because they been at it longer. These fellows with us, now that's a different matter. Course, I'm just an old paratrooper, but that's how I see it."

"You know, I ain't goin' to buy that rubber tonight. I wanted to talk it out some. You know, you got to have some when you're over here a year, but I want to be back with my wife. I've brought her lots of surprises. She's goin' to really roll her eyes. Hell, what I really wanted to do was talk it out. It's goddamm good to talk."

"There's a fellow in my outfit, he got killed couple weeks ago. He was a real good fellow, he was my friend, but I guess I think of him as kind of a hero, yes, I guess I do. I mean when they got him he'd used up all his ammunition."

"Master sergeant's best. Sergeant-major takes it from everybody. I reckon they ain't nobody gonna keep me from bein' master sergeant. I figure E-6 this year, then 7, then 8, yeah, I'll make it."

"Some of the fellows say I don't look out for them enough, well, I can't wipe their noses for 'em. I'm at it all day tryin' to get our job done but I'll see two of 'em promoted to 4's before I leave. One of 'em's a cruddy bastard, a real slophound, but he's good, I'll put him up for it, he'll have a good chance. Hell, if he don't make it, it'll show him not to be so cruddy."

The nightly rain. Curfew and the white-uniformed police patrolling all the streets. We separated to hit the sack. He had work to do. I put down some of his words.

Steam Bath

Why couldn't he leave Tangier? He examined his thin lips, thin nose, blue eyes, two lines above his bony eye ridges, and short loose-lying blond hair. When he hiked his lean blue jeans through the outlying villages, bearded Arabs laughed under their peaked djelabas and occasionally he heard the Spanish "como mujer".

He lived in a European hotel on the side of the cliff where he was known as the "Americano rubio" and treated with deference although he was only twenty-three. He loved the palaver of the British over their drinks and the way they behaved exactly as British expatriots had been described by British writers. They spent an hour bringing out a nuance of anger from a rich bitch and another hour sending over drinks to the straight-laced Scottish woman who didn't drink.

But each day, he wandered more and sipped more mint tea. Each day he found new side alleys and some sweet new cookie to munch upon. Each day he found new Arab hustlers pushing keef, pot, majoom, hash, or themselves upon him. Some were young and smoothfaced and their gold teeth gleamed. Their hands extended to lie softly in his to greet hello or say goodbye.

People ate at any and all hours. Loaded burros, donkeys, horses, women, men, children paced through the Zoco Chico and Arabs, Americans, Britishers, Scandinavians, who knows what, sat endlessly drinking mint tea or café au lait, watching, watching, watching. Like Burkhardt's Florence, no two men wore the same costume. The women flirted with their eyes, the blue gauze veils provocative. Some of the young, pretty ones gathered their gown around their buttocks as they walked, flashing their dainty ankles and Parisian spikes.

He no longer wanted to tour Europe. He was one of those who did not know why they stayed, but who could not leave Tangier. He learned the exact prices of the sweet juice-filled oranges and ate a kilo a day.

Finally he took a steam bath. Handed a bucket of hot water, he threw it on the wet floor. His clothes safely locked in his own cubicle. No steam arose, but a certain warmth began to diffuse on the floor and between his toes. An Arab boy, about eighteen, came in and sloshed his bucketful on the floor. He eyed the Arab sideways, but the Arab looked him over boldly. Heat rose in his cheeks and his head turned and cavorted like a flirting girl's. He could see the Arab's penis rising. "No, no," he murmured, but could not keep his gaze from the dark hair and unwrinkling skin.

"You want me?" the Arab demanded, flicking out his hand to touch with the sure gesture of a mechanic placing his wrench for the thousandth time. Shriveled and small, he backed away. How was he suppose to take him? Anally or orally? Oh come now, asshole or mouthhole. He shuddered.

"Come on. Come on. I good fuck." The Arab reached for his penis again and though he turned, the Arab's hand curled over his hipbone. What would happen if he lingered just a trifle more slowly in his moving away?

"No, no! Get away from me. Get!" A dog. The Arab like a dog after him. "Get. Get away. Get, do you hear me?" His voice chattered in his ears, high, excited, alien. "Please!"

The Arab grabbed his own penis with his right hand and began back and forth, back and forth, while the Arab's left hand still groped toward him. He kept backing and crouching but stayed close to the Arab, unable to take his eyes from the back and forth, back and forth hand upon the uprisen flesh.

The Arab stopped pursuing him and stood in the middle of the wet floor, scrunched his head back on his neck almost down between his shoulders and gaped his mouth. His hand flew mercilessly back and forth on the perpendicular flesh. White jets exploded out, arced, and wriggled into the wet film of water on the floor.

The blood began to pour out the distended flesh. It drizzled out steadily, splashing and spreading onto the wet floor. My God, I'm glad I didn't. God in Heaven, I'm glad I didn't. My God, I'm glad I didn't.

The Arab boy's hand loosened to a finger hold. He looked down at the blood drizzling out of him and then up. "I sick, yes, man, I sick, huh?" The Arab's lips slacked, tried to smile, then slowly slacked again. The brown eyes stared straight at him as if afraid to look down again at the red drizzle. Wouldn't it ever stop? The Arab boy's stomach sucked in and he could see the Arab's skin stretching over his ribs. He must be too frightened to breathe. My God, he must be scared.

"Yes. You're sick. Don't worry. Doctor will cure, — Doctor will fix up. Understand? Doctor. Doctor will fix up." He looked around. Water tap. Cold water, congeal blood. He picked up the bucket and filled it. The threw it on the read drizzling upraised flesh. Freeze, you bastard, yes, it's cold, but it's got to stop. Driving me nuts, your bleeding to death, sick. God, I'm glad I didn't.

The Arab retreated, hands trying to protect his shriveling flesh, stopping forward from the blow of the cold water. His brown eyes seemed to keep pleading, though, for help of any kind, no matter how painful.

Step around the blood. Careful of my cut foot. "Need more cold. Stop blood!" He finished throwing the cold water on the Arab's fast shriveling flesh.

"Taxi. Taxi. Take taxi to doctor. Doctor will cure. Will fix up."

The Arab squatted and began pissing water. At first half-red, half-yellow, then became all yellow. The yellow spread over the floor and he pushed himself against the wall trying to avoid all white and red and yellow splotches.

The Arab smiled dully, shaking his head forward and backward. "I go to doctor?"

"Yes, you go to doctor. He will fix."

"I see you again?"

"No. No."

"You help me. I see you again?"

"No. Oh alright. Tomorrow. Zoco Chico. At noon."

"I see you."

"Alright. Get to the doctor!" he screamed.

"Okay, man, I go doctor." The Arab left, smiling dully.

All the stuff all over the floor. Who'd ever clean the place? Infection everywhere. Careful with his cut. He hopped on his uncut foot to the water tap and refilled the bucket. He sloshed the water out on the floor. Drive all the white, the yellow, red splotches down the drain. Drive them all away. Drive it all away so there's no infection left.

The Research Lab

The harsh electric buzz of the controller at fifteen second intervals, the glaring electric lights, the white aluminum paint on the furnace, the low hum of the revolving black-spindled screw feeder, all combined, without malice, of course, to produce in my mind an hypnotic-like state of suspended time.

Every hour measurements had to be taken. In this one operation lay all the virtue of the laboratory; this alone connected vision and reality.

What difference did it make if we made mistakes, if our accuracy on any given reading was meaningless because of unpredictable fluctuations in the operating conditions. This mistake would be on one side of the truth, the next mistake on the other side. If we but noted down the conditions, holding them approximately unchanged while performing enough trials to overcome any probable run of mistakes in the same direction, the plebeian law of averages would make the patrician truth emerge, untouched as it might have been on any single trial.

The fingers at work in the research building, although distinct, were almost ghostly: Joe, tall, lean, red, whose long fingers curled around a wrench with familiar mastery, who called people "uncle Jim" or uncle Bob," a tight-skinned grin stretching over his bony face; Mike, short, stout-shouldered, a small pot just beginning to jut from the lower part of his belly now that he was fifty, slow-moving, slow-talking, never wasting a motion in his work, conserving his energy as carefully as though he were still on the production line, always ready to stop and joke, yet getting as much or more done than anyone else; Alec, hulking, making the tough energetic motions of a football guard, thick-glassed, his doctor's degree in physics only a year old, nervously enthusiastic in his desire to make a quick 'name' for himself; Roy, also an engineer, almost furtively poppng in and out of sight, reticent, serious, a painstaking calculator; and so many others.

Why did they seem so shadowy? They were intelligent, had led varied lives, loved, doubted, and sought answers to puzzles of their existence; still, like the protectively tinted jars lined on the shelves which nonreactively held the most potent chemicals, they seemed to have the wild surges of their blood, the harsh eccentricities potential in their brain, safely stored away. Perhaps it was the quiet, apparently effortless control that had caused them to lose the crowding substantiality of those lives which must, at least on an occasional Saturday night, taste the savage vigor of the flaunt and search.

Maybe it was that the research company gave them such a good deal, and they knew it so well. The company had no time clock, so they arrived a little late and left a little early. The company had to sell accurate predictions; to gain these, it had to have, within certain limits, accurate measurements; therefore its employees were left to work at their own speed which they set themselves by a compromise between their own skill and their own interest. The company did pay only medium wages, but the pay was certain; there were no strikes, no layoffs.

No woolgathering was allowed, however. The engineers did not idly flush the sponsor's good interest bearing money down the drain. There were no wild goose chases after some fantastic theoretical truth; metaphors were bad, mixed metaphors unforgivable.

A calm life spent at a healthily moderate rate of work, geared to the practical needs of great American corporations, guaranteeing a certain amount of novelty in their daily routines, a comfortable wage, social respectability, it nonetheless demanded and obtained a certain price: the almost ghostlike thinness which was their memory and their passion. This price had the advantage of being exacted from willing customers.

Hans Miller, Wobblie

I

Hot. Clear California blaze on Highway 99. The Sierra Nevadas like blue storm clouds to the east; all the other directions flatter'n a pancake far as his eye could roam, here just south of Fresno.

A stream of diesel trucks and shiny new cars hammered past him at 60-70-80 miles an hour.

Half-a-mile down the road stood a grove of dusty green olive trees. Grapes covered the countryside with their low orderly rows. A few tall eucalyptus trees, bark hanging loose from their trunks, formed a parody of a country lane along the sides of this superhighway on which he walked slowly northward.

The big man, stopped now with age, Dutch jaw still square, eyes a faded blue, kept his white whiskers trimmed in the sturdy spade style. He travelled in a simple costume: grey pants rolled-up a couple of turns at the cuff, a uniformly wrinkled shirt under a brown suit coat, a flat-topped broad-brimmed hat, ankle-high shoes that he kept open at the top, tying the strings below the hooks at the last eye-hole. A light blanket roll fitted on his shoulders.

Reaching the olive orchard, he looked suspiciously about. No cops or owners in sight. Heaving a capacious sigh, he pulled a huge red and white bandanna from his rear pocket and mopped the sweat off his high forehead.

His old legs just didn't have what it took any longer I days past he could laugh at thirty mile. He chuckled as he made his way over to the shade; eh, the old days when a man had the kick of a stallion in his legs I he'd enjoy himself then in spite of it all. Aches were something to laugh at then I yes, well the world was no place for an old man who just cluttered it up, a man that somehow never got around to having time to marry and have kids, why should he expect anyone to care what happened to his old carcass?

He leaned against the trunk of one of the trees. The sandy bottomed irrigation ditch was pretty dry, about time for another watering. Dirty green old trees, don't stand out enough to be really ugly drab old trees, like an old man.

He took a pipe out of his coat pocket, then a bag of tobacco, carefully untied the bag and shook the tobacco into the bowl of the pipe. An old man who's lonely learns to make his private rituals; they make some kind of friend.

He pressed the tobacco down with his fingers, lit the pipe and took a long easy puff, then sent the white smoke sailing gently past the shade to vanish in the sunlight.

What was it that tall lanky kid used to tell him about olive trees? He could never work, always bumbling around, eyes and see not, ears and hear not I just out working around from college for a summer.

Those olive trees, Hans, his voice rang out, are the most beautiful trees on earth I on olive trees Athens and Florence grew.

Athens and Florence I and what or who are Athens and Florence? Great cities of art and science, whose fame outlives old doddering working men cast off by each generation. We old men die but Athens and Florence made possible by olive trees shine brightly forever.

Son, he had asked, did they live off the olive trees or off the men grew and harvested the olive trees?

Why, Hans! You're not half dumb! The kid laughed.

Eh, yes, well he could still chuckle in his pride at that I sure surprised the boy.

One time in Frisco he'd even gone into the library and read Aristotle on Politics I the olive trees had turned out something there all right.

By God, Lincoln and Marx and Jack London and Grapes of Wrath were good, too I but what's the use? Men still starve and work their guts out, drink a bottle of wine, and run to a cathouse. An old man remembers many failures I not expected to have any fire anymore. Just expected to die without causing anyone trouble.

Aye. Enjoy the shade. Puff the pipe. A lot of hard walking from here to those strawberry patches at Portland, Oregon. Don't want to hit that old freight unless I have to. Too old, too old for that.

He careful knocked the tobacco out of his pipe, hitting it against the sole of his shoe, then stowed it away.

The highway was a little more crowded, more roaring, speeding, vanishing noises throbbing out the vast strong pulses of commerce, the sun a little hotter. The old man hiked painfully down the road, and yet the rhythm of the walk, the sweat that loosened his muscles, the surrounding heat, soon reduced his consciousness and he, too, like the trunks, like the sun, the endless rows of grapes, existed a thing impersonal, a silent changing numeral in nature's multitude.

II

A pick-up screeched to a stop. "Hey, get in, Pop!" A lean frazzly red-bearded, fox-faced man yelled out.

"Well, yes I will. Thank you. At last a ride.

The driver was an intense young fellow who wore a T-shirt and blue jeans. He was gazing steadily at the road.

The fox-faced man was of an indeterminate middle-age, face lined with wrinkles, his eyes devouring with an apparently open curiosity the passive hitchhiker. A half gallon of wine jar was between his knees.

"My name's Elmer Wilson," he said. "This here's Jed Smith. What's your name, dad?"

"Hans Miller."

"From Holland I or Germany? Well, I fought you Krauts the first time. Have a drink, Pop?"

"Look," the driver broke out, "You promised no more drinking till we got there."

"Sure did, but we got a guest I and we got to be hospitable, you know, don't we?" Wilson gurgled down a sizeable amount of the cheap red fluid.

"Where you goin', dad? We're headin' to Sacramento."

"I'm goin' to Portland."

"Well, you gotta good lift here. Have another drink."

The old man ordinarily didn't drink much but this was a good long ride. No use to spoil it. The two men he was riding with had some kind of tension and he didn't want involved.

"Now, look," the young man, Smith, said, "When you see Governor Warren, it's not just to tell him we don't want amy more Mexicans across."

"You C.I.O. boys got it all figured, don't you? Well, listen, we don't want no foreigners in here, do you see? That's my union's plank, and by God, we'll see to it they don't get in. They're the American workin' man's enemy I low pay, long hours I here, have a drink, pop."

The Elmer raised the jug and lowered its level another half inch.

"I don't see how you do it, Mr. Wilson. You had five beers already."

"Keep in practice, son, keep in practice."

"Say, Mr. Miller, were you ever in the old IWW?" asked Jed.

"Then damn Communists!" snorted Wilson.

"No, they weren't, but they were a fightin' bunch."

The old man sized them up I well, the Wobblies were a long time dead. No hurt to say a few words.

"Yes, I was in the Western Federation of Miners I logging camps I some people says they went too far, but by and large, they did a lot of good."

There was a lot of good fights in the old days I there wasn't anymore though. Everybody sold you out once he got in office. A young man had room for a lot of hope but an old man had it all kicked out of him, had all his bigness of outlook shriveled down to enjoying a puff on the pipe, the luxury of well-salted, well-peppered scrambled eggs fried by a clear creek, the hope that winter would wait a couple of weeks longer this year before it started chilling. An old man was a being squeezed of his vital forces, squeezed to the meaningless outside of society, to hang around until the coyote dragged his away into the night.

"Were you in that Cripple Creek fight?" asked Jed.

"What was that?" Wilson interrupted.

"The greatest mining strike ever fought," came the brusque answer.

"Yes, I was. Right there in Victor, Colorado. Yes sir, forty seven years ago."

"Listen, were you guys scared when they sent those troops in and started arresting everybody?"

The old man leaned back and smiled. Those had been the days! He was in his early twenties, could speak good English too I that was how he got a good $3.00 a day job without scabbing. They had been scared just a minute when the army moved in but I

"We were madder than we were scared."

"I don't see how you fellows held off. I get so mad reading about it myself I could blow my top. But that's what they wanted you to do so they could arrest all of you."

"Sure was, young man. They'd ride up in a big cloud of dust and take some poor fellow off to the bullpen from his dinner table or even out of bed."

"They called concentration camps bullpens then, Elmer."

"You're right about that, son. There was some of us hot-headed but we never started a thing. They had to start it all. They arrested the whole staff of the Victor paper and the women folks got it out just like always."

"Listen here," Elmer said, killing off another drink, "you mean to tell me here in America, an army came in and just took over? Why I'd get my gun out so fast . . ."

"Look, Mr. Wilson, it was this way." Jed began explaining.

The old man looked out the window toward the blue Sierras nearly lost in haze. A poetic thought came very unexpectedly on him I he was no hand for poetry but he recognized this thought as something different.

The mountains of my past are lost in haze too, but they're still mountains.

Oh those were the days of Bill Haywood, Gene Debs; then came the Wobblies, the bitter starving winters after the first World War; men shoved out of fast moving freights with only an oath onto the vast Dakota wastes. And the last stand I how well he remembered it. Just a tiny group stood gathered at Yakima, Washington; then came the rumor they were all going to be tarred and feathered.

And somehow there in that beautiful valley of apple and pear and cherry orchards fierce knots of violently talking men gathered on a low ridge west of town.

"The workin' man has got to stand up and fight someday and it might as well be now."

"They want us to take twenty, fifteen cents an hour. We're men, not beasts."

Oh, a lot of big talk, some of it even kind of wild and beautiful but they all knew they were licked. But they gathered there hoping, hoping. Yes, there had been mountains in his life too big for him to understand.

Some of the men picked up stones and branches.

And while they were standing there the orchard men, the vegetable men in the lower valley, the hop men, the chamber of commerce men, had gathered their shotguns and pitchforks.

"Make an end to the Wobblies!"

"Show those foreign bastards this is America!"

Come on outa that field and help us," they yelled to their men working for even ten cents an hour, twelve hours a day. "You a red, too?"

The men on the ridge crumpled a little inside as they saw the oncoming mob but somehow they stood firm. "Fight 'em, men, fight 'em, stand up for your rights," a little sawed-off fellow ran around begging. Hans remembered standing there with only one rock in his hand looking at the enemy with an ache and wonder in his heart that they really meant to break his skull. "Brothers, brothers," he kept repeating to himself.

"All right, you dirty Reds, come on down or we'll take you down," somebody yelled.

"Workers of the world, unite!" one voice rang out but that was all.

"Jesus God, they're gonna kill us," he heard the man next to him sob.

Then two shotguns went off, and there was a lot of yelling, a big charge, everybody running, he remembered standing, frozen with disbelief, until a burly farmer, brandishing his shotgun, got within ten feet of him. He started to throw the rock, then smiled, dropped it, and something smashed over his head.

So many things in life you had to be silent about. How could he express what all the misery and hate and love had meant?

And after that everything seemed rather useless. Still this young man, who was out doing things, remembered. There was bound to be others. An old man didn't get around.

He remembered the waitress, a pretty redhead she was, too, at Victor after that old strike. "You're a hero, Hans!"

"Well," he'd said, embarrassed, "I have to go on to Utah and help Bill organize."

This young man knowing about Cripple Creek bucked him up. Maybe even if society squeezed you out where you were worthless, maybe even then some of the things you had done, if they were good things, lived on.

"Mind if I roll down this window a little more, son?"

Sunbright, the air flooded in fresh and saucy.

Lena

Red Parker had promised me an introduction to Lena ever since we'd decided to leave the potato fields and headed north to the timber country around Willets.

"I been hot for that woman for ten years," he whined in a slow drawl.

Red stool tall and lean; between his weekly shavings a frizzly beard flamed on his chin like a lit match. His sparse hair hung in hay wisps over the front of his ears; his blue eyes peckered around like a rooster in a grain patch. Somehow, Red kept a dignity. He was forty years old with nothing in the bank to show for it, but he kept the kind of dignity that the scrawniest, mangiest wildcat never loses.

His rain, grease, and dust-stained hat, always pulled down across his forehead, caused and protected a triangle of white flesh that he rarely revealed.

His old brown suitcoat slouched over bony shoulders. Half laced-up boots, faded jeans, and a half-unbuttoned shirt completed his usual wear. His skin, like the sea, was nowhere smooth; wrinkles radiated from his eyes, and razored down his cheeks. He'd been reared in the east Texas hills, the kind of man you don't want to get in a fight with.

Red liked and went after the good things in life, as he had learned to know them, women (including the one he had married), whiskey, young men around (including his two sons and myself), a tuned-up engine that'd take him where he wanted to go, a hard game of poker, and a winning fight.

So when an east Texas white like Red kept telling me about a forty year old Negro woman he'd been trying to lay for ten years, I felt like breaking down the barn door to meet her. She sounded like a legend, and I've always wanted to see a real, live legend. I believed in them, but, at twenty, outside of my grandfather who'd died ten years before, I had never seen any.

We were only making seventy cents an hour picking potatoes anyway, working on the Old Guy's place that summer of 1950. Ten hours a day crawling after the racketing and uprooting tractor, shoving potatoes in a gunny sack, then four hours more heisting the sacks onto a trailer I healthy work if you're healthy, but not much fun, so cutting timber sounded like a deal. Red said he and I'd go up first, and if there was work, he'd write his sons to follow.

"Besides," he said, "On the way, we'll stop by the old homeplace and I'll introduce you to Lena."

We drove out to her brother's. A pile of junk, two pickups, and several rolls of fencing formed a wall around his cabin. Big Boy stood about six and a half feet tall; he wore a black two inch wide leather belt, T-shirt, and jeans. He could have picked Red up with one hand and flung him all the way out to the road. "Hi, Red."

A woman, a gypsy scarf turbaning her head, emerged behind him onto the planked porch. A good natured grin stretched Big Boy's face; he nodded agreeably to some talk of Red's about renting a truck if such-and-such should happen. But I had been brought to meet Lena, and standing only three feet from her, seeing her bare shoulders broad as mine, hips to birth a clan (though she was childless), her smooth face, I felt my fingers itch to touch her.

Red had told me that she and her brother each year led a hundred people over the state, chopping cotton, and picking cotton, oranges, lettuce, and carrots. Neither the brother nor the sister had finished a sixth grade education, but, from Red's account, they ruled their tribe with a just hand, buying, selling, trading, building, trucking, and planning.

"Where do you live?" I asked Lena.

"Over there." She pointed to a cabin about a hundred yards away. Her bare full arms did not have a trace of flab, nor did they have the cordy muscle of a man. I wanted to know her more than I wanted anything on the green or desert earth or both combined. More than a bankroll or a willing blonde.

After we left, I jumped on Red. "I thought you were taking me to see Lena. All you did was talk to Big Boy."

"Son, you got to get acquainted first. She knows your face now. You can look her up when we get back from Willets."

I didn't like the idea of waiting another two days, but Red, a lean package of bone and muscle for all his slouch, was definite.

He insisted we stop at his wife's house that night so he could try and make out with her. At his direction, I set the alarm at six so we'd get on the road.

"My God," he yelled when I pounded on their bedroom door as instructed, "I've spent the whole night talking to this woman and feeling her up and just when she's ready, your alarm goes off," except, of course, Red's actual words took twice as long to say because he coupled every noun with a violent mechanical obscenity.

His wife, an Indian, padded out of the bedroom in plaid shirt and jeans. She never looked at me, but I noticed she filled her jeans pretty nice. Red must have married her when she was fifteen or sixteen. She put out coffee and eggs and bacon and pancakes for us. Red and I fell to on the eating, and then we took off without them hardly exchanging a word.

It was raining that afternoon when we climbed into the hairpin curves of the Coastal mountains. I drove hunched forward, the road was slickery, and rain now and then gusted so thick the wiper wouldn't clear the windshield.

"You're drivin' good," Red told me.

"Yeah?" I was relieved; I had been thinking how much an effort I was putting into driving, secretly picturing Red doing it very relaxed, one hand on the wheel.

"You ain't putting the wheels across the center line. That's okay."

The thing that bothered me more than the rain, though, was Red's drinking. He had finished a bottle of wine in the course of the day, and now he started on a pint of gin he'd stowed in his hip pocket.

He told me like it was an ancient story how he'd been in the Texas penitentiary. "These boys had stole my hog. I got my gun and set out after 'em. I wasn't meanin' to do anything, just scare 'em and get my hog back. But they was waitin' for me, and they tied me up by one foot, and hung me face down in an old well. I got loose and went after 'em again. When I caught 'em, I killed 'em. It was simple justice."

Red delivered his story with many obscenities and several pauses to drink, but he didn't put any embellishment on it.

"How'd you get off?"

"Saved a guard in a fire." he said. "They turned me out, but said, don't you ever come back to Texas."

Though the rain finally stopped, the clouds made the evening chilly and black as tarpaper. "You got a nice lookin' wife," I finally said. "How come you keep going after Lena?"

It had taken me all day and nearly six hundred miles of driving to work up the nerve to ask.

"All women is good," he said, "but some are special, like Lena. She never let me make out with her. I'd go over and talk to her a long time, help her and Big Boy get lined up on a ranch job sometimes, but she never let me."

"Didn't she ever get married?"

"Never did, no." Red's chin sunk down on his chest. He'd finished his gin and passed out.

At last we reached Willets. I decided to drive out of town a ways so we could sleep without being waked up by a cop. I drove slowly down a side road by the edge of an irrigation ditch, pretty tired myself. Red's irregular, groaning snore began to scrape my nerves.

"Hey!" I shouted at him. This did no good. I leaned over to shake his shoulder a bit. Then I noticed a two inch hang out of his nose. It swayed every time his head nodded. At another time it might have been funny, but now it quickly became infuriating. I looked for a place to park off the road, but there wasn't any yet.

I looked over at Red and got madder and madder. Bent over, he looked like a dirty, unshaven scarecrow with the straw about to come out. His head flapped, loosely waving the hang from his nose. His lips slobbered half-open. Willets was shut down for the night, it was a hell of a lot smaller burg than he'd led me to believe, and I wondered if there were any jobs besides dishwashing in the drizzly place. And Lena! Hell, of course she'd never been interested by this filthy drunk by my side, or if she had been, what kind of a woman was she? Certainly not a legend.

Suddenly I knew I couldn't stand that waving hang from his nose any longer. At least that didn't have to be there. I shoved him, all respect gone. He wouldn't wake up. Finally, I jerked at a handkerchief in his pocket, and then, smash.

By reflex, I braced against the wheel, but with a slow-motion sickness I saw Red pitch forward and crash his head into the windshield, the whitening spread of the cracked glass.

We'd nosed into the irrigation ditch. Only one rear wheel stayed on the road. Red came up as from a dive, bubbling for words, about the time I had recovered to catch his shoulders to pull him back from the glass. I hugged him in spite of the nose hang. I had been worried for him and worried about a manslaughter charge for myself. Now I was only worried about the pickup.

"What in hell did you do, boy?" he growled. But we both got out, Red taking off his hat to feel and prod around on his head, and surveyed the pickup for damage. It was only hurt at the windshield where Red banged his head.

I got mad again. "Wipe your goddam nose," I said. "That'll cost me twenty bucks to get that windshield fixed. That's thirty hours on my knees pickin' potatoes." I cussed worse than Red usually did, partly because my knees felt weak.

"That's no cause to run a pickup in a ditch," he said.

I left him standing there, still half-drunk, a bump on his head, and hiked toward town to get some help. A two-and-a-half ton rolled by, but the brakes slammed on when I waved. Two big fellows sat inside wearing sweatshirts, one, the driver's sidekick, with a beer gut. They drove me back to the pickup and they broke out a chain and pulled us out of the irrigation ditch. Then Red and I leaned back and slept about three hours till the sun came up.

Sure enough, no hiring in Willets for loggers.

We started back toward the potato fields, neither of us talking much. I was irritated because I had built up hopes of getting logging work, and Red had one hell of a hangover. What with the bump on his head, I imagine he ached.

When we reached his hometown late that night he said, "Let me off at my wife's. You go down and tell the boys to come up here. I ain't pickin' no more potatoes this year, and they ain't either. You come on up with 'em, if you want."

"I don't want. This whole trip didn't get me anywhere. It just cost me gas for twelve hundred miles and a window."

"Tell 'em I told 'em to pay you for the window." He turned and hiked into the house. I hated to see him leave. He'd got me the job with the Old Guy and I'd eaten his scrambled eggs and bacon and drunk his hot black pan coffee in the mornings and swum with him and his sons in the irrigation canal at night. I knew I probably wouldn't see the old bastard again.

And it was too bad about Lena. I wanted to meet her. Then it hit me. I was going to see her. I wasn't going back to that potato patch and work sunup to sundown for the Old Guy another couple of weeks and cuss myself out for not seeing her.

It was midnight, and it took me till one o'clock to drive round and round that town's outskirts till I found Lena's cabin. I parked the pickup on the edge of the road and looked over at the dark cabin for a long while. Down the road about a hundred yards I saw Big Boy's cabin, and beyond that several smaller shacks. The clear sky was full of stars.

Finally I started cussing myself. "Haven't you got any guts?" I said out loud. It's queer how you talk to yourself to work up the nerve to do some things. You sort of sit like a flat tire, but you want to roll, so you talk to yourself like a tire pump building up pressure, and finally you move. Makes you wonder what else is in you besides yourself.

I tiptoed up on the porch, quiet enough so I could back out anytime before I knocked. Everything was dark. I couldn't hear a sound.

I knocked on the door. Then I knocked again, harder.

"Who's there?"

"Me," I said. That was all I had to offer, Me. She'd just have to come out and take a look to what she thought.

Minutes seemed to go by. I heard bedsprings creak slightly, and the frictional soft grit of feet on a wooden floor, and at last the door cautiously opened. I had my hand on the screen door handle, so I knew it was latched. I could scarcely make out her face at first.

"What you want?" she asked.

"You remember me. Red brought me with him."

The door opened a little wider and she studied me through the screen. "Alright. But what do you want?"

"I want to see you. I want to talk with you. You look like a gypsy queen with that turban on." I was surprised and pleased how fast I talked.

She chuckled. "I ain't no gypsy queen. Let me put a light on."

She lit a kerosene lamp, down low, and then opened the door and unlatched the screen. "Come on in," she said.

I came in, and we stood facing each other. She was barely shorter than I was, and I wore boots while she was barefoot. A cotton nightgown hung straight down from her shoulder to calf. She was bareheaded, and her hair kinked close to her scalp.

"You wanted to talk to me," she said.

"Yes."

"It's pretty late at night to talk to someone."

"Sleep with me," I said. "Ever since I heard about you, and saw you, I want to sleep with you." I frightened myself. I had not admitted this to myself before. I wanted to get acquainted with an interesting, romantic character. Sure, a guy can hardly help a quick daydream now and then, but this was the first time I'd ever come right out and known this was what I wanted. Now I was in her power. She could laugh at me, drive me out, call her brother.

She looked at me long and carefully. "I don't know," she said. " I hardly know you."

"I know you don't sleep with just anybody. Red told me you never slept with him."

She laughed. "That's right. I don't know why. That old buzzard, I like him, but I never want him. I got him a girl to sleep with now and then, but he always wanted me."

We stood silent again. I felt like a beggar, but I was too full of need to care. I felt like my eyes and mouth and shoulders and arms were all imploring.

"I don't mind helping a man out when he's hard up." she said finally, "but I don't think I should do it for nothing. How much you give?"

I was furious at myself, and her. I wanted her to do it for me, not my money. I had nearly twenty dollars left, but I wasn't going to give her half of that and feel like I was buying a whore. I pulled what I had out of my right front pocket. I'd put the last gas change there, two crumpled dollar bills and a fifty cent piece.

"Two-and-a half," I said.

She laughed and turned away.

I put down the money on the windowsill. "There's two-and-a-half. Hell, it ain't much, but I want you."

She picked the money up, counted it, and looked at me. She turned off the kerosene lamp. "Come on," she said.

I was clumsy, in a hurry to get my clothes off. My boots thudded like thunder on the floor. I felt sweat prickling out of my chest.

She was a big woman. I fell into her arms, and we began to wrestle. She was a strong woman. We wrestled for several minutes.

Her shoulders were as hard as mine. Her long breasts fell loosely this way and that. Her skin was smoother than anything I'd ever touched, except maybe a baby mouse. Finally, we both rolled over on our backs, side by side, and laughed like old friends.

I kissed her. She had a sweat smell from the wrestle. I had never felt anything as soft as her skin.

"How can your skin be so soft?"

She pushed her belly up against me, pleased.

"It's as soft as a baby's, soft as a corn tassel, softer'n that even."

"Well, I never had a baby. But I'm forty years old. I used to be softer."

"Couldn't have been any softer."

We kissed some more and we stretched the length of ourselves against each other.

Suddenly, I was ashamed. " I don't know what's wrong. I can't do anything."

We worked and worked for some time but nothing happened. The joy drained away from me. " I don't know what's wrong with me."

She touched me reassuringly. "Nothing's wrong with you. You probably just want me too bad. That's why you can't."

That was true. I knew it. But I had never hoped that she could understand. I, who had gone to sleep rigid after fourteen hours work in the potatoes, knew, but I could've gotten worried. I needed her to reassure me.

My worry and sweat went away. I held her close and tender, and she held me. It was like we had been lovers a long time. She understood me.

For I don't know how long we talked, lying there close and relaxed. She told me that women ought to be allowed to fight in wars, "I can shoot as good as any man," and we talked of Red, and of how she ran the commissary side of the business when she and Big Boy took to the road with all their group, of how she arranged marriages and affairs.

We became restless again, and wrestled and kissed and embraced and fondled. "You've got me hot," she cried at last and I felt with shame that she was imploring me as I had implored her earlier.

Then, yes, it occurred. The black happiness came.

The room began to grow grey. She rolled over on her stomach and pointed out the window. There was considerable light above the blue-dark ridge of the Sierras.

"You've got to go," she said. "It's nearly six o'clock and Big Boy'll be up soon."

"I don't want to go."

"Why don't you get a job around here and see me again?"

"Maybe I will."

Outside, the air was fresh and cool from the desert night. I drove eighty miles, almost back to the Old Guy's place before I had to pull over and sleep for a while. My eyelids clamped down on each other.

I was going to be smart for once in my life and never see Red or Lena again. It was funny, how they were both connected together in my mind. In some crazy way it was almost like giving up a mother and father. I felt immensely free. Like when I stopped going to church ten years before.

Sun, even through a pickup window, and sleep, though I was sprawled out crossways on the cramped front seat, never felt better.

Skid Row

I

"I'm Bill. I reckon it don't make any difference where I come from, I have lived in every little pimple hole of the carcass of America." He shook Tom's hand with limp, reddened fingers.

"Don't bother that guy lyin' there on the snow, first thing you learn here, buddy, if a guy's killin' another guy in front of you, don't lift a finger, don't lift an eye, keep on walkin'.

"It's just askin' for trouble to butt in, understand? Sure the son-of-a-bitch's bleeding but what're gonna do about it? You got a bandage? You got a car to take him to the county hospital? Cop come along and see you messin' with him and you'll get three months in Bridewell. Not for me, no sir."

Tom Mulden was new to Skid Row and these terse answers chilled him but he didn't feel man enough to go against this cynicism that rang of truth; so he didn't lift the dirty, unshaven, slobbery-lipped head off the ice, not even momentarily in order to put something around it. He was repelled by the filth of the head, and frightened by the blood freezing on the smoke-dirtied snow. Something yawned hollow inside him, empty, where all of his ordinary emotions had disappeared. He wanted to, had thought he did feel love and friendliness for other men, but there seemed no place for emotions like that on this terrible street.

The cold cement stairway casually doubled back and forth up six stories, never heeding the panting men, frail with age and drink, who sat down to rest at the turns, gazing into dimness.

Rows of little cardboard-walled coops stretched down his half-block room. Chicken wire protected the top of his six and a half feet high coop. Vomit and cleaning fluid mingled caricaturing a hospital smell.

Men coughed and coughed, till he thought their vitals would be torn loose from the racking torture. "Shut it up, you bastards!" others screamed at them in sleepless frenzies. "Shut it up! Shut it up or I'll kill you!" Animal howls of anger built to screams that drowned out the coughing. Even he began to curse at these destroyers of his sleep.

"Why don't you hurry up and die?" one voice flung out disdainfully to a cougher, and he hoped the voice said it only because there was no chance for any cure in The Working Man's Palace, as the hotel was called.

Human life was sometimes very cheap, he saw, and he could not explain why it became so. No one here had time or energy or purpose to care for anyone else, and no one had enough money to pay people for taking care of them. He was not fascinated by Madison Street, how easy it seemed to him for some big magazine to carry a story on the Salvation Army, for a big shot to drive his Cadillac through the Street and enjoy slumming! Why, the Street was so colorful it was a Chicago tourist attraction like the Lake! But to live there as he was doing, a runaway of eighteen, it was not colorful, only cheap. And it was not too cheap, he thought, when he was plunking down his thirty and forty cents for a tasteless meal.

His people had always worked with their hands, but he wanted an education. So he had come to this brutal and powerful Chicago, that fall of 1949, living on twelve dollars a week, saving thirty-one dollars a week, sustained by a fanaticism he hadn't known he possessed. In a year he would be able to go to college.

Oh yes, it's possible, he wrote his mother. He did not write her how he bought day-old bakery goods at half-price, how he ate only certain sausages, or meats like pig snoots for his supper meal. He walked to wherever he was going for he had time and patience. And he wore jeans and sweat shirts for work. The only price he had to pay to live so cheaply was to live on the Street. It was not too cheap.

His new friend, Bill, was only twenty-seven but he had the wisdom of an old man corroded by the lies of a century. He would eat with Bill, occasionally walk "downtown" with him. The Street was never called "downtown" although it, too, was a canyon of tall buildings. Nothing, it seemed, escaped the cynicism of Bill's tongue. It was a cynicism which lashed out at all things, bad and good. Tom liked Bill because of this cynicism. Most guys on the Street could no longer muster this much spirit.

"Yeah, there's nothin' to get worked up at here. Why they got a place like this everywhere." Almost with a note of pride in his voice, Tom thought, just like national parks. "Why, Phoenix, L.A., Oklahoma City, Houston, Toledo —I been around. They're all the same."

Walking "downtown" they'd cross the little river, maybe stop and look at the ice floating down it, dirt with coal smoke like everything else, and then they'd walk by the City Opera House. "Bill, we ought to go to the opera sometime," and he'd reply, "Hear them dames bustin' their lungs open screechin' loud enough to deafen ya—not me, kid, not me. Bottle o' wine do ya more good than a dozen of them things." And Tom could never make him go. He had to see many so-called cynical people before he realized that this attitude helped them bear their lot. How many "cynics" there are in these United States not all by a long shot on Skid Row! And yet even while he felt sorry for Bill, he wished everybody would stand up sometime and say "Dammit, we demand to live a good, full life!" But how were the cynics ever going to demand something they had never got a chance to see, except now and then, unless instinctively dreamt from their desire for life? He himself did not know what a "good, full life" meant.

II

The giant train whoo-whooed through the night leaving Chicago I South Chicago, Hammond, Gary, back there in the black. Leaving the heartland of steel, of power, wealth and revolutionary machinery, leaving the swelling impoverished life of the strong people of Chicago back there in the dark.

In Tom's car a pudgy drunk reeled on plastic legs. "Come on and fight. Come on and fight. I'll knock your damn face in."

"Aw, come on, Pop, sit down, sit down."

"I'll knock his face in.

The back door of the coach opened and the boss man stepped in. "Hey, cut it out, what the hell do you think's going on in here? Cut it out, break it up."

The men sunk in their seats. Lights flashed red off the bottles of cheap wine that was slipped into a vest.

The boss man walked up the aisle glaring at the conspicuously averted faces.

All twenty-three of the men had jammed into the dingy Baltimore and Ohio office on West Madison. "Laborers Wanted" was blazoned across the dirty window in white paint. There was only a counter, a couple of long benches facing each other, a dish and two chairs behind the counter, an indifferent clerk and . . . the twenty-three men. An empty, undecorated, brown, dusty room with a lonely steam heater coiled greyly against the wall. They had all been told to be there at 7 p.m. The big clock on the rear wall showed 7:30, 8, 8:15. The agent kept scribbling. No one ventured to complain except one big red-haired unshaven man with the shoulders of a bull, who was told, "Wait till I get word."

At 8:30 the clerk, who had spent fifteen minutes joking with an old crony, oblivious of the twenty-three men waiting for a chance to earn their food and clothes said "O.K. Get down to the station. Train leaves at nine fourteen for Timbers, Ohio."

The station was nine blocks away. The wind hurled icy rain stinging into the cheeks of the men.

They bowed their necks and trudged forward, a black-coated silent caravan, shifting their bags from hand to hand now and then. Tom wondered if they could each possibly be as cold as he was. They all lifted their heads erect when they reached the help of the grim dryness underneath the high pillared sidewalk, roof of the Union Pacific. Only two voices cursed the company for not providing a bus.

The train pulled to a stop in the middle of Ohio in the chill of early morning. Red light seemed frozen to the top of the low wooded mounds to the east, as frozen as the hard brown ground the men dropped on to. No porter, no conductor got out for them. The boss waved his cotton-gloved hand to the engineer and the train chush-chushed off to a metallic roar of speed.

The gandy camp in front of them was two long buildings at the outskirts of a small town; three blocks away a big two-story white house stood alone like an indolent well-dressed woman in the middle of some bare oak trees set back from the combination highway-main street.

The men trudged up the wooded ladder steps into the bunk house; the other building was the mess hall.

"Hi! Fresh meat!" yelled a huge black-bearded man who sat half naked, legs dangling, on a top bunk near the pot-bellied stove cherry-red from blazing wood.

"From Chicago?" "The Madison Street Gang!" "Oh you Winos!" The men inside sat up, stood up, or walked over to investigate the newcomers. One or two saw old acquaintances. "Damned if ever'body don't hit Madison sooner or later!"

Double bunks were stacked closely together all down the room, in the center, wherever there was space. Only the rookies among the newcomers stopped to talk, the veterans rushed to grab the cleanest beds or the beds closest to the stove.

"How's chow?"

"Oh Holy Lord!" It stinks!"

"What's it matter to you, Wino — you got along without eatin' on Madison, didn't ya? Where's yer bottle?" Everybody laughed.

A tinny bell clanged and rattled.

"Chow's on!" Tom pushed and crowded with the rest of the men out of the bunk house for the mess hall.

Burning hot, water-thin soup, hot, thin coffee, listless scrambled eggs, whites still half liquid, were slammed down in bowls, pitchers, plates. The men fell to.

"Did you see that cloud in the Northwest? Gonna snow like the devil today."

"Do you think we'll work today if it snows?" Tom, a first-time gandy, asked.

"Work?" "Hell, you work harder to keep from freezin' to death! Yaw, Yaw I" "Like great bellows Tom heard the annihilating laughter pumping vitality into men who saw things from the bottom.

"We get a hot lunch?" he asked.

"Son, where'd you come from? They didn't pick you off o' Madison, did they? Carry out some coffee and sandwiches."

Clouds slid like a shutter across the sky to cover the pale sun; the ties between the tracks were frosty white. The men put on whatever they had, two pairs of stockings, old sweatshirts, torn suitcoats, leather jackets, hats, mittens, gloves, looking curiously alike in their variety, poverty and hopelessness uniforming each one.

And yet as they split into two crews, as they picked up their crowbars and sledgehammers and spikes and rail tongs and lifted them expertly, as they piled onto the hand cars and the truck in a calm, confident, orderly manner.

As they set out to repair the iron sinews of America, to lay the steel into the frozen flesh of winter Ohio in order that the industries of Cleveland, Akron, Toledo, Youngstown and through them, American be served, in order that the hog and corn growers transport their goods to the cities . . .

As he went with these huddled, uniform figures to the work, Tom felt their confidence infused into him, their sense of mastery of their tools and nature warming them and him.

And Tom Mulden working with the men from Skid Row suckled on the wine dregs of Gold Coast-Madison Street America, felt increased power to resist the windy bitter snow that began flaking downward, sifting into his collar, falling over the frost-rimmed steel tracks.

III

Two men, one lean, with sly wrinkles around his shifting eyes, the other fat and broad shouldered, walked down Madison Street with an arrogance seldom seen on Skid Row. To their backs, in the West, the sun was a blazing red over the grey piles of buildings. The red glared evilly over their black-suited, white-collared backs; Tom thought they seemed ministers of hell with their dead fish eyes and unspeaking mouths.

The men of Madison Street slunk cautiously against the sides of buildings as these two figures approached; wine bottles were slipped under coat arms; all became silent as the two men strode down the street. Tom Mulden felt hate flooding him, walking behind the two men, watching them ever more closely.

One old man tipsily walking westward, weave to his steps, perhaps to him the red sun a faint reminder of red-winged blackbird chirping in South Dakota wheat fields, if he remembered anything. A faint smile of being at peace with all humanity played around his lips, a peace bought at the price of expecting nothing.

On he walked toward the middle of the black-suited men who walked shoulder to shoulder, the sun diffusing its smoke-barred red between their ears and shoulders, leering almost in anticipation. Tom's stomach crept backward; he hated even himself.

The two men halted. The broad fat man spun the old man with a blow to his shoulder.

"Look where you're goin', bud!"

Fear hit the old man's eyes, the peace he bought at such a price fled I he knew no price that could obtain him peace. A streetcar roared by to the west. A few eyes glanced sideways down the street.

"I ain't doin' nothin'."

"Tryin' to talk back, huh?"

Tom did not know what made him act. He could do nothing else. He spun the stout man around with the flat of his hand. Grinning, the two men grabbed him, nearly breaking his arms. Badges shone with evil enlightenment. "Interfering with arrest! Come on, you." The old man slunk into a side door.

Hurled into a black car, the red sun almost gone, the squad car sped Tom into the grey dusty dusk toward Racine and Madison.

"Name! Address! Occupation!"

"A bleeding heart for those winos, huh? Don't you want us to protect you?"

"See this whip! By God, be careful the next time!"

The sergeant half-risen from his seat, stout and menacing, smashed the rubber hose on his desk in fury.

Into the long block of cells they poured behind Tom — the prisoners of the law, the to-be-punished, the guilty, the criminal, the winos, the inheritors of the great Anglo-Saxon tradition of fair play.

Square cells, regular bars, he couldn't see to the side, a slab of concrete on steel bars, two of them, beds for six prisoners. Toilet without a seat.

All during the night they were shoved in. Finally eight men packed the cell with Tom.

"I'd just bought a pint of wine."

"My old man's a minister — Jeezus, I just came to Chicago and then this guy took a poke at me in the bar, tried to steal my wallet, we hadda big fight so the police come in and said, "Come on, Assault and Battery.' Jeezus! My old man —"

"I'm tellin' you, I was just standin' in the toilet, havin' a piss and smoke when this kid comes up and asks me for a smoke. I give 'im one, the owner and cop they comes in and says I'm puttin' the make on the kid. Colored man ain't got a chance. I thought they'd get my dough but I had it in postal notes."

Piece of bread in the morning, cup of coffee shoved though the bars.

"When in hell do you see the judge?"

Two pieces of bread, hunk of salami at noon, cup of coffee.

"They can't keep you here but seventy-two hours."

Two pieces of bread, hunk of salami at supper, cup of coffee.

"Yeah, but they send you out the door, arrest you again and start another three days sometimes."

"They must be yellin' about no law enforcement in Chicago again. Some of them Citizen Leagues. Break up the gangsters!"

Four old ladies stood in front of the cells. "Repent, for the Lord forgiveth all crimes."

"Don't piss in front of them ladies. Show some respect." But the musical splashing continued.

"Hallelujah! Hallelujah!" Tom's ears roared with confusion flashing as bright and meaningless as jukebox lights.

"Yeah, they gotta make more arrests or the coppers'll look bad this month — look like they ain't doin' nothin'!"

"Hallelujah! Hallelujah!" The four old women sang, their faces, as calm as if God stood by their side.

Alone

He scrambled up the last few feet to the top of the cliff. Snow-covered peaks looked flat as a cardboard cut-out on the southern horizon. At the base of the cliff, the dark-green Columbia slid windingly between lava banks on which apple trees, white-leafed from spray, grew in thick orchards. And straight across the gorge he breathlessly saw Lake Chelan stranded eight hundred feet above the river.

Finally he turned eastward where the wheat flamed yellow over the tops and sides of all the rolling hills on the plateau. He couldn't help but sit down and look and look again from direction to direction. Red Dog had bet him three bucks he wouldn't make it to the top, but he had; he had made it to the top, and now he had to go back down again to the crowded bunkhouse and the old men with unshaven grizzle and the young men with their slouch and whiskey, back to propping and thinning the apple trees before they were overcome and broken by the weight of their own fruit.

He had to climb back down, but it was hard actually to give up his lonely view, his powerful survey of the jumbled mountains to left and right, the broad Columbia, the hanging lake, even the dusty sunburnt wheat that spread up and down the hilly miles so monotonously for so far that it, too, became splendid. That was the trouble about climbing, he thought, you make it to the top and then you have to climb back down again. It was the clearest philosophy he had ever thought out for himself, and it impressed him nearly as much as his physical achievement.

Reluctantly he began his descent. Huge boulders of lava, tamaracks, and jackpine soon cut off his sweeping view. Then a little lower, the mountain itself dispersed into small regions divided by great gulches plunging dryly toward the river.

The deep breaths of sage-scented air which he drew in dispelled his sadness. After all, he, a boy from the plains, had, by conquering this rocky summit, laid claim in a certain manner to most of central Washington in that brief but satisfactory manner that his frontiersman forefathers had so well understood.

He walked faster, finally speeding into a trot, braking and sliding when necessary on the steep descent. The ground levelled off for a way, and he broke into a run. He strode to the top of a rock, and took a great step from it. Mountain goat couldn't do better, he thought. A wild cry burst from his lips.

His eyes misted over to protect themselves from the wind made by his running. He hurdled over jutting boulders, lunged over sagebrush. The glory of the run made him reckless of his strength. He had to gulp in scalding, heaving air, but he kept pounding downwards, now carried as much by the slope of the mountainside as by his legs. He cleverly swerved and turned to follow the sharp contours.

He was to the slight cliff before he saw it. From the distance its twenty-five or thirty feet had not been noticeably worse than the rest. He saw he couldn't stop, and with desperate insight tried to throw himself around in the air so that facing the cliff he could clutch the edge with his hands and arms.

A rock smashed into his stomach, then his shoulders and head bounced against something hard and tearing, then there was a snapping fall, a long almost lazy roll. Pain fired in waves from his back, each new wave engulfing the last. He felt shapeless, sprawling, but the pain gave him no time to be sure of these sensations. The pain seemed like an outside force holding him down; he couldn't think he was holding all that hurt inside.

Finally he spun into a vortex, conscious only of dizziness and dull spasms.

The sun was still warm when he opened his eyes. One of his cheeks lay flat on the ground. The sagebrush just in front of him was greyishly purple; small white and brown rocks were scattered in the small space that he could see. The sunlight seemed almost buoyant, but still he couldn't move.

His ears came unstopped, and he learned that he was groaning; then he felt the spit trickling out of the corner of his mouth nearest the ground. Vaguely, he wanted to lick the spit away, but he couldn't move his tongue.

He tried to move his fingers. They raked weakly over the sand, hardly displacing a grain. Anyway the pain's gone, he thought. He sweated and felt like a warm blanket was wrapped tight about him.

Wonder when the boys will get here, he thought. Old Red Dog knows I might of come on up. Then he remembered the store clerk would be absorbed in his Sunday whiskey and game of blackjack. The Mexicans would be playing the guitar and doing their little hop around a sombrero, or talking of las mujeres and los politicos. Like every Sunday afternoon. The mountainside would get cold when night came.

The pain throbbed again. He started to swear, then began moaning. The pain gradually lessened.

Suddenly he thought he might die. It was an empty, stupid, stubborn thought. He felt fright pass through him, like he'd seen shivers go through a wounded rabbit in the pasture. It was stupid to die from running down the side of a mountain, stupid to die because he had felt too alive to walk cautiously down the cliff like an old man.

He screamed. The scream was so loud it frightened him even more. He screamed again and again. The pain increased.

Finally he was silent; he felt the sharp grains of sand grit not only against his cheek now, but also against his lips and nose. He didn't try to change his position.

It was easy to kill a hog, he thought. You took him out in the open and put a bullet between his eyes. Then you ripped his throat open, and the bright scarlet blood gushed out on the barnyard where it took a couple of days to sink completely in. The blood just made the barnyard richer. Cow turd and the straw over stable floors, the water that spilled out the tank where the catfish were kept when they were caught too small, scattered hay from the wagon, and the chicken eggs that were laid under the barn or in the hay beneath the trough and were occasionally smashed; all these, like the pig's bright scarlet blood made the barnyard richer in memory, in color, and in smell. There was at least something about a hog's death that lived on after it, he thought.

Of course his father and mother would remember him; he pictured the stout woman's body shaking with grief and was a little consoled.

He'd been aiming to get a farm, marry a girl, build a barn. That was when your life meant something. When you had a home, a barn, and some children. You could go fishing almost any time you really wanted to except in the plowing and harvesting. You could sit on the mud bank and look at the fireflies, listening to the water of the Washita. When the moon was up at night and rippled over the water or shone white off a sandbank sticking up or soft and mysterious through a willow tree with the sky all blue around it, you could sit on the bank and think about all the things you had ever wanted and all the things you wanted still.

They used to fish for crawdads in Polecat Creek by the old Thompson place when he was a kid. They caught a lot of minnows, too. They seined for whole afternoons and the lay back in the sun to dry out.

The panic was worse, a great useless hurting. It was hard to keep thinking. Why should he keep thinking, he asked himself. He wanted only to forget the pain. He'd felt good so long ago; why had he ever run down the mountain?

But the questions were peaceful. He had climbed the top of some mountain, that he remembered, yet now a sweet sage scent was filling his consciousness, an exultation of some conquest, yet a strange eagerness on the return, on the coming back down.

Now he was running again; some terrible cliff was barring his way, but still he was running eagerly down sunlit gulches plunging toward a dark river. He ran and there was joy in the running though he was going down and he did not want to go. He ran alone and forever there would be joy in his running.

Comraderie

He was going to see *Hedda Gabler*. He had looked forward for a week to seeing the 4th Street Theater production. He prided himself on keeping up with serious theater.

He arrived at the theater an hour early, stood expectantly for a minute or two, and then realized that he was only waiting for the crowd to arrive.

He decided to walk around the corner to Third Avenue and have a beer. As soon as he walked in, the long, old, wood-paneled bar, he liked the place. There was no television on. Two stout men, broad shouldered, about forty, wearing scuffed leather jackets, played the pinball machine. Their women, butts slopping off the bar stools, talked animatedly over their drinks. One of them was white-haired, but rouged and lipsticked as if ready for action. The two bartenders were big guys over six feet tall; they looked like brothers, like ex-bouncers who had bought a place of their own. The dark-haired one pushed him his glass. He liked the way the bartender was friendly without saying a word,

In the corner booth, a Jewish man and his girlfriend, both wearing dark-rimmed glasses, talked forcefully to each other, interested in making their points. They were in their late twenties and their lips curled knowingly although their eyes flashed.

He sipped at his beer. He had not felt so alone in a long time. He should have brought some girl, maybe Marie, to go to the play with him.

A Negro slammed the door and staggered into the bar. The men stopped playing their pinball machine to stare at the Negro. He felt himself, in a judicious way, that the Negro was out of place. The Negro was obviously drunk; he muttered; he swayed when he tried to stand still. It was not a question of race, he thought, but of the Negro's being a bum. After all, to be really unprejudiced one had to admit that Negroes could occasionally be in the wrong, too.

"Get on out of here," the dark-haired bartender waved his meaty arm at the Negro as at a fly.

He made up his mind that the bartender was justified. He liked the people at the bar. None of them was interfering with his drinking. The Negro had no right to disturb them with his shuffling and muttering. Same of a white drunk, of course. It was clear-out.

The Negro drew his long grey overcoat tight around himself before backing out. He remembered it was zero outside, bitterly cold under a clear sky. Well, the Negro would have to find his way back to his flophouse.

To his surprise, the bartender suddenly strode from behind the bar. A small Negro with flat cap pulled down over his ears turned to face the bartender. Apparently nobody had seen this Negro come in. "I'm just goin' to the toilet. I'll be out in a minute."

The small Negro did not mutter or sway. The bartender grabbed the back of the Negro's coat and shook him once. "Get out; you hear me?"

Hold on, he said to himself. This Negro is not drunk.

The bartender began pulling the Negro out. The bartender tugged the sleeve of the Negro's overcoat over the Negro's hand. "Get your hands off me, white man!" the Negro cried out.

"Come on, get out, get out." The bartender kept pulling the Negro. They were nearly forty feet from the door.

"I'll go. I'll go. Only get your hands off me. No white man's got the right to touch me." The Negro struggled.

The stoutest man left the pinball machine. He began kicking the Negro.

"He's got a knife! Watch him, Joe, he's got a knife!" Her hind-end tensed on her stool, the white-haired woman turned to watch the affair closely.

The Negro lunged with his one free arm toward the stout man. The bartender groined him neatly, and the Negro's head jerked forward. The stout man came at the Negro again, kicking him, and hitting him in the face. "Trust a nigger to use a knife," he shouted over and over.

The two white men dragged the Negro out the door. Nobody talked inside the bar while they were outside. He thought, I have to do something. He thought of calling the cops, but figured the people in the bar would frame the Negro. The other bartender went over and picked the knife up. It was a pocket knife. The blade was out; it was rusty and bent at right angles at the tip.

I'm holdin' this here as evidence," the bartender announced to no one in particular. He laid the knife down behind the whiskey bottles on the shelf in front of the mirror.

The two men came in from outside. The dark-haired bartender turned the radio up. A fox trot blared out.

"He nicked me on the neck," the stout man said.

"It's only a bruise." The white-haired woman drank from her glass.

"I broke my little finger on that nigger," he said. He gave a tentative wiggle to his finger. "I broke my finger on him."

"What'd you do with him, Joe?"

"Threw him in the gutter, whatta you think we did, pat him on the back and send him home?"

The dark-haired bartender made a motion, as if asking did he want another beer. He shook his head, no.

He stood up. The Jewish couple were back in the swing of their conversation. Love, he thought, insulation.

He hurried out the side door. The Negro lay stretched full length on the sidewalk. Down the block he saw the signs for *Hedda Gabler*.

He turned the Negro over. The dark face was congealed with blood, the forehead and left jaw were swollen and split.

He picked the Negro up. A drunk Negro watched him from across the street. I didn't do it, he wanted to shout. I only want to help him. At least a little. How in hell would, could, any Negro tell a good white man from a bad one? He was almost afraid.

"Thanks, man," the Negro said.

They proceeded slowly down the street. He put one hand gingerly under the Negro's shoulder to help him walk, "You got a home?" he asked. "You got to get some alcohol and bandage that thing up."

"It hurts, man, it hurts. It's started to hurt."

"You got to put some alcohol on it." They moved slowly down the street. There was bound to be a drugstore on the next avenue. What was he going to do with the man? Swab alcohol on him and take him home, perhaps? What more could he be expected to do?

What more would be any use to do? The signs for *Hedda Gabler* were now directly across from them. He wasn't going to see the play now. Fine. He was no longer interested in her suicide in her big rich house. Tomorrow perhaps. Tomorrow he would be interested again.

He knew he would undoubtedly never see the man again. They walked slowly together, his hand under the man's shoulder. "I want to thank you."

"Don't thank me, you'd do the same for me, if I was in your place."

"I would, man. I would for a fact."

He looked at the man's brown eyes, his busted and bloody cheek, his dirty overcoat. He thought there was just a chance that the man really meant what he said.

The necessary
Transform coordinate
System for freedom
Is the Wild.